AF556344

The God Who Loved Motorbikes

The God Who Loved Motorbikes

Murali K. Menon

JUGGERNAUT BOOKS
KS House, 118 Shahpur Jat, New Delhi 110049, India

First published by Juggernaut Books 2019

10 9 8 7 6 5 4 3 2 1

This is a work of fiction. Any resemblance to persons, living or dead, or to actual incidents is purely coincidental.

P-ISBN: 9789353450595
E-ISBN: 9789353450588

For sale in the Indian Subcontinent only

Typeset in Adobe Caslon Pro by R. Ajith Kumar, Noida

Printed and bound at Thomson Press India Ltd

For Snigdha

1

I first saw the Norton Dominator, the motorcycle that changed my life, on a miserably wet night. I was a little past the bus stand in Kollengode, walking around in the rain, when I saw the smudge of a headlight and heard the muffled roar of an exhaust note coming at me from afar. There was not a soul around except for the bike, its rider and me. Then, in an instant, the motorcycle whipped past me and thundered into the darkness. A little curious about the mystery rider, I hurried after it, past the post office, the Thangaraj theatre and Kollengode's many houses and shrines.

I instinctively knew who the rider was when the motorcycle slowed down at the entrance of the lane that led into Azhakappadath house. Who else could it be but Koman Kutty! There he was, standing under the cover provided by the many trees in the lane, taking deep drags of his Scissors cigarette and admiring the motorbike. Koman rolled the bike into the courtyard of his home after finishing his cigarette, parried his mother's admonishments for getting back home at that wretched hour, and took one last look at the Dominator before heading off to sleep.

The Dominator was parked alongside the veranda, with the last ten or so centimetres of the house's sloping, moss-encrusted roof affording it some protection against the elements. It didn't look new to me, but it was handsome and pretty big, much bigger than any of the bikes Koman had brought home before. There was nothing Koman couldn't get away with, I thought, as I lay down on the wooden bench in the veranda, and hoped, as I always did, that this was one of those rare nights when sleep would bloody come early.

When I woke up the next morning, a brooding empire of clouds still hung over the village, but the first rays of light had seeped through, and they bathed the Dominator in a kind of other-worldly luminescence. I sat up and – this was highly uncharacteristic of me – gazed at the beefy British motorcycle. Now, I don't know whether that was the tipping point, but for the first time in my life, I wanted to viscerally possess something. I wanted to get astride the Dominator, feel its engine erupt under me, wring that fucking throttle open and go riding on a long, winding, endless road.

I remember feeling scared of myself. Was I turning into a rabid lover of motorcycles? Would I be spending the rest of my life talking about acceleration times, clutch adjustments and blown gaskets? What the fuck was happening to me? And why? I still don't have an answer to the second question, but that is exactly what happened. One fine day, some sixty years ago, I woke up and found myself lusting after motorcycles, and my life since then has been mostly about motorcycling. Now, Kollengode's pious dicks would have considered it to be god's wish, but I don't quite agree with that. At this point, I think, introductions are in order. My name is Kandakarnan Swamy – call me KK if you find my name a mouthful – and I am a village deity. I was 'installed' in Kollengode, in central Kerala, a long, long time ago. My village is surrounded by cobalt-blue hills and there are paddy fields and lush coconut groves, but its good-for-nothing men have fermented breath, and the women, mostly fat and ugly, are so gossipy that should one sew their mouths up, their tongues would wag out of their ears.

I, or more accurately, the concept of Kandakarnan Swamy, it is said, came in through Tamil Nadu, which lies to the north of the village, as part of a

Shivaite wave that saw many of the Bhootaganankal have godhood thrust on them. The Bhootaganankal, and that includes me, are supposed to be Shiva's hangers-on. Once, many years ago, I actually tried to delve deeper into my origins and discovered, to my own great consternation, that there are hundreds of different representations of Kandakarnan Swamy across Kerala, including a corpse-eating clown, and almost ended up with a multiple personality disorder. Like Shiva, I, too, am symbolized by the stylized phallus, or the lingam, but this one's rather cursorily defined as compared to the idol that represents the big boy.

There was a time when nearly every family in Kollengode worshipped me. Those guys prayed to me before they sowed their fields and the invocation of my name preceded the worship of many other significant deities. Kollengode still has homes where I'm worshipped fervently. And twice a year, on moonless nights, some of these sons of bitches gross me out by sacrificing a rooster or a goat – sometimes, it is a simultaneous affair, with the rooster made to perch on top of the goat – as this violently writhing, bloodied token of their gratitude. So, you're wondering if I'm a minor village god who is also, as outrageous as it may sound, a motorcycle enthusiast?

Correct, but I am not your regular minor village divinity, and that's not just because I am mad about motorcycles. Thing is, I'm not sure about this entire god business. I mean, what I want to know is, do I exist because my devotees think I do? In this unflattering form of a stout, dark-complexioned man with long hair, a grand, upturned moustache, and with golden danglers, and anklets that are supposed to go 'jilm, jilm'? Or, am I literally here, an entity independent of the feverish imagination, anxieties and hopes of a thousand human beings? Am I fucking there or not?

It's kind of complicated, and I don't really foresee an alleviation of this metaphysical anxiety any time soon. But for the last four-odd decades, I haven't had much time to agonize over it, and that's because of this other thing that has laid siege to my imagination, and defined, as it were, my existence. Kollengode usually throws up enough distractions during the daytime to help me take my mind off it, but the longing becomes unbearable once the sun sinks below the hills around the village.

Every night, I assemble the Velocette Venom Thruxton HT, the greatest motorcycle ever made, in my head, and each day a new machine emerges out of it. And then I rev it up and savour the roar from its fishtail silencer that probably lingers in the air like an aural spoor. I've been told that a motorcycle such as the Thruxton HT cannot exist, and it could very well be true, but that hasn't stopped me from searching for it all these years, and if I do find it, I hope to be more than a match for it.

2

My transmogrification into a motorcycle nut was swift and brutal, and I'm glad I didn't stand a chance of resisting it. Upon eagerly straddling stationary motorbikes in and around Kollengode and nearby Palakkad and going 'wrooffffffff, wroooofffff' on them, I discovered that they opened up a world of sensory experiences to me.

I could touch and feel motorcycles, an ability previously restricted only to palm leaves and then books and later computers. Reading has afforded me great pleasure if not clarity on my condition, but it is, at best, second to the joys that motorcycles periodically populate my desolate life with: the touch of rain, the warmth of a fire on a cold night, and the rough embrace of pine-scented wind. I'd go so far as to say that perhaps I exist when I ride. And back then all I wanted to do was learn to ride. That was how Koman came into the picture.

Koman was the youngest son of Krishnan Nair, a tall, brooding man who built Azhakappadath house in the 1930s. His wife, Ammini-amma, gave birth to nine children, seven boys and two girls over twelve years. I don't recollect much about the other kids, but Koman was a strapping, handsome lad with a perky moustache when he was young. He was exasperatingly mischievous as a child and grew up into a reckless young man with a glad eye and a gullet that imbibed great quantities of liquor.

I was always fond of Koman and his closest friends, CK and Gopalan, but I really took to him after the Shivan Kovil incident sometime in the late 1950s. Shivan Kovil is a biggish shrine in the centre of Kollengode. It was, and still is, tended to by a Brahmin family that zealously guarded its territory. After a particularly heavy monsoon, it was decided that the shrine needed major repairs and everyone in Kollengode, from the raja to Karuppan, the coconut-tree climber, was encouraged to contribute. The raja gave some fifty rupees in an uncharacteristic display of generosity, while several ingratiatingly pious Nairs, Menons and other landowning folk chipped in with varying amounts. Even the village's lower castes got wheedled into parting with some of the little money they had for the benefit of a god that was not theirs. By the time the monsoon winds weakened, the temple committee had collected a tidy sum, which was put into an ornate vessel and 'offered' to Shiva for his blessings. This pointless ritual was conducted the night before the masons were contracted, and the money was left behind the shrine's rickety doors.

It was on that very night that Koman and 'Gunda' Gopi felt that all that alcohol they had imbibed deserved to be chased down by a grand meal. The problem was they didn't have any money. Koman, about nineteen at the time, was beginning to discover the pleasures of alcohol, both the local variety and the more elusive, branded 'English' liquor. He had filled the vacuum left behind by his childhood pals – CK and Gopalan spent most of their time in Palakkad; the former was a junior staffer with the collectorate and the latter in college – with another set of friends. 'Gunda' Gopi was one of them. Gopi and Koman were sworn enemies at first. Their bloody, no-holds-barred brawl in Kollengode's Big Bazaar was for long considered the gold standard for slugfests by the village's shopkeepers and merchants, but the two soon developed a mutual admiration for each other's spunk and bonded over their love of a good tipple.

It was nearing ten that night when Koman and Gopi stepped out of the toddy shop.

'The hunger, Koma, the hunger, I could eat a horse right now,' said Gopi. He was relieving himself by the roadside.

'Hmmm . . . I hear the Shivan Kovil committee has collected some money for repairs?' said Koman.

Gopi told Koman that the committee members had approached him, too.

'I gave them eight annas.'

'Don't you wish you had it now? We could have gone to Ayyappan Nair's hotel. Imagine a meal of sambar, rice, and some mackerel, or sardine fry? Do you think Shivan would mind if we took some money from him?'

'Koma! You prick! Have you gone mad? You'll invite a curse that will last for generations.'

'Da, how much will it cost to repair that temple? Not more than two hundred rupees. Where is the rest of the money going? To those cock-sucking priests and the members of the temple committee.'

'I don't care where it goes. We might be drunkards and rogues but we are certainly not thieves!'

Seated on a milestone by the road, I was party to this heated exchange between the two. Ultimately, it was decided that they would head to their respective homes, drink lots of water, and eat a hearty breakfast the next day. But Koman being Koman was not finished yet.

'Da,' he said, 'let me ask you something: have you ever seen god? Where are all these guys? These Krishnans, Vishnus and Shivans? Who told all these donkeys they need a bloody temple and all these offerings? There is no such thing as god. All this is just another way of making money from fools like you.'

Gopi glared sullenly at him and walked on. Koman stood swaying on the edge of a rice field; he was still spoiling for a fight.

I was no stranger to such pronouncements. Eventually, after feeling hurt for a long time, I had come to terms with the fact that there would always be folks who would make you feel like shit and that, despite the uncomfortable implications it carried with regard to my existence, they had a point. So, while I admired the boom in Koman's voice, I also wondered how long he would hold out. Would his ability to question the status quo wear off the next morning, or perhaps a decade or two later, especially when he got knocked about by life? To his credit, it never did. Koman glowed with that militant conviction right till the end of his life, even when it was painfully ebbing away, and throughout it, religion and gods were a source of great amusement for him.

'How can these idiots believe you exist when you yourself are unsure of whether you do?' he once asked me. All I had to offer in response was sheepish laughter.

So Koman called out to Gopi and said that they were not stealing the money, just 'borrowing' it.

'How's that?' he said.

'Koma, call it what you want but I won't be party to this.'

'Okay, I am going to the Kovil. All alone . . . da Gopi, all alone. You hear that? Without my best friend. All alone,' Koman said. He was a clever bastard.

Gopi turned around.

'Don't talk about friendship, Koma; you do what you want, I'll wait outside,' he said. All his life, the bugger always held out these grudgingly tacit approvals of Koman's wild plans.

And so, on that dark night, Koman squeezed himself past the gates of the temple, snapped open the flimsy lock on the doors that led to Shiva's hallowed chamber, 'borrowed' five rupees from the container that held the money, and walked out.

Kollengode went berserk when the theft was discovered. There was talk of all sorts of stuff befalling the people who had committed the horrific crime. The matter ultimately died down, but Gopi was wracked by guilt and never failed to remind Koman about the money he owed Shiva. And each time he did, Koman would flash an impish smile and tell him, 'I'll give him his money when he asks me for it. Shambo Shiva!'

For a while I thought Koman would waste his life away, especially considering the time he spent at toddy shops as a young man, but about three years after he passed his tenth standard exams, he, sort of, got his life back on the rails. I think his favourite sibling Ammu's sudden divorce had a lot to do with it. Ammu's marriage hadn't lasted long, but it had yielded a bonny girl called Parvati who always clung to Koman's little finger. Like in the movies, Koman took it upon himself to take care of his sister, and his, as he would often say, fatherless niece, and I saw him change overnight. He enrolled for his pre-degree education at Palakkad's Victoria College and then sat for a junior officers' exam held by the Kerala health department. He cleared it easily and earned a posting in the sanitation department at Palakkad. He would rise to become the health inspector of many districts in Kerala, get transferred numerous times because he brooked no interference from politicians in his work, and retired as a pretty high-ranking state-level officer.

Koman remained a man of his word at home. He looked after Ammu and Parvati until he got his sweet niece married off to Chandran, a tall, handsome export manager working in Bombay. But he never left alcohol – literally drank himself to death – and it remained as addictively integral to his life as motorcycles.

3

Back in the day, the only notable bikes in and around Kollengode belonged to Kadar 'Mechanic' Moideen. I mean, if you had a Royal Enfield Interceptor (the early 1960s Series 1 model) and a BSA Road Rocket, why would you even bother with the more ubiquitous Bullets, Jawas and Rajdoots?

Kadar was an intimidating, taciturn man, unless you were talking motorcycles with him. The guy lived in, and worked out of, a tiny home near the bus stand. He was the one who introduced Koman to the joys of motorcycling, and, quite naturally, Koman paid him a visit the evening after he got the Dommie home. He rode the motorcycle into the courtyard of Kadar's home and revved it hard.

'Kadaretta, how's it?'

Kadar dropped the newspaper he was reading and hastened towards the motorcycle.

'Koma! I heard!' he said, adjusting his spectacles.

'I was thinking of dropping by. How did you manage it?'

'Aaaanh, it's from Thrissur. Belongs to a sahib who's moved to Bombay. His mechanic is a good friend of mine, and he's asked me to keep it until the sahib calls for it. I'm hoping it will be with me for at least a month.'

'It's beautiful, but careful, Koma, this is a 650SS, so don't try your usual stunts on it. This one can really go!'

'Yes, I'm learning something new about it every day. Very different from Bullets and all,' said Koman, who was then employed as a clerk in the district health department in Palakkad.

'Appo, Kadaretta, we should go riding – your BSA versus my Norton. How about early morning tomorrow before I leave for work?'

That bit about the Dommie's imminent departure from Kollengode made me stop vacillating about introducing myself to Koman, and, convinced that extreme intoxication would help him be more receptive to abstract concepts such as myself, I ambushed him the following weekend when the two friends were making their way home from the arrack shop.

'Koma, Gopi, how are you?'

'Who's that? Koma?' Gopi said.

'What? I told you not to have that last glass . . .' said Koman. He tottered along. His eyes were shut and he had a smile playing on his lips.

The road we were on was bordered on both sides by rice fields and up above us a squadron of monsoon clouds blotted the moon out.

I cleared my throat and told Koman that I needed to talk to him.

'I need some help.'

A startled Koman looked around. 'Who's that? Who are you?'

'Aiyyo, run! It's the poltergeist!' said Gopi. The two friends hitched up their mundus and took off.

I gave chase and pleaded with them to stop running, and ultimately, I caught up with Koman who was about two yards behind Gopi.

'My friend, I am no poltergeist or ghost, I mean you no harm,' I shouted into his ear.

Koman swatted the air around him, swung his hands wildly and kept running.

'Koma, Gopi, I am Kandakarnan Swamy. Wait, please listen to what I have to say.'

Gopi froze on hearing my name. Koman, who was now a few yards ahead, turned around and animatedly gestured to his friend to move on, his body poised for flight. A mongrel barked in the distance, and, soon enough, other strays around Kollengode relayed the baton of suspicion.

'Swamy!' Gopi prostrated on the ground. He continuously changed the position of his outstretched hands, trying to pinpoint the source of the 'divine voice'.

'Da, do you want to get killed by this ghost? Get up and run, you prick!' said Koman. He ran up to Gopi and tried to lift him off the ground.

'Swamy . . . Kandakarnan Swamy, I had told Koman there would be consequences if he stole the money from Shivan Kovil. I know you have come to punish us for that. We were kids then, please spare us,' said Gopi, awash with penitence.

'Da Koma! Fall at the feet of the lord and tell him you are sorry. And you are returning that money tomorrow, do you hear me?' Gopi berated his friend and simultaneously yanked at Koman's shirt, bringing him sprawling to the ground.

I was breathless after all that excessive exertion, and Gopi's petrified piety and the bickering between the two friends grated on my nerves, but I was also acutely aware of the fact that this was the first time anyone had responded coherently to me. Long used to being treated as a symptom of a diseased mind, including by those who claimed to be my most ardent devotees, I was not going to let this opportunity go. I composed myself and quickly got the situation under control. I told the two this had nothing to do with the Shivan Kovil incident.

'Friends, please just forget about that,' I said. 'I want to talk to you about something else. But first, why don't you get up from the middle of the road and sit down by the side?'

Gopi sprang up. Koman lay there for a while looking unsure, before joining his friend by the side of the road.

'What is it that you want from us, Swamy?' asked Gopi. His head was bowed, his palms were joined.

Koman's lips twitched in annoyance.

'I don't mind helping you, whoever you are, but god doesn't exist – any god, big or small. Whatever is happening right now is because that rascal Ravindran must have given us something spurious to drink.'

'Koma! Will you shut up?' said Gopi. 'Forgive him, Swamy, he's a madman.'

I had anticipated just such a seemingly insurmountable obstacle, and my plan was to step right around the 'god' debate and atomize Koman with something even more ludicrous than being stalked by a god. This was a god with a special request.

'No, Gopi, your friend is not entirely wrong. I had expected just such a response from him. In fact, I myself have given this question much thought, and I have to say that after so many years, I'm none the wiser,' I said. 'But, Koma, right at this moment, there is something a lot more important than the issue of whether I exist or not. So, let me come straight to the point: I want you to teach me how to ride.'

Koman froze, and then burst out laughing.

'Da Gopiiiieeay, what is this guy saying? I think that Madhavan is using a loudspeaker and trying to fool us. That pig is constantly thinking of ways to get back at me. But this was a good one: a god who's not sure whether there is a god and who wants to ride motorcycles. Class!'

'Koma, Madhavan has gone to Salem to look for a job,' said Gopi.

'Then it's someone else. I've had enough of this, I'm off,' said Koman, and proceeded to get up.

'Wait, Koma, I know it's difficult for you to understand all this, but all I want to do with my life is ride motorcycles. Ride hard, and ride long, and ride all kinds of motorcycles. Please hear me out and then decide whether you want to help me or not,' I said.

Gopi hissed at his friend. Koman assumed his previous position, and I proceeded to tell the two friends the story of my life. I thought I was especially voluble, but then it felt so good to talk to someone. My story ended with the day I woke up in the morning and saw the Norton Dominator with new eyes.

Gopi took Koman aside. The two friends argued for a while. Then Gopi turned around and addressed me.

'Swamy, my friend here still thinks it's the liquor that's doing it. But he is also confused. He says he is willing to help–'

Koman cut right in. 'Whoever you are, you obviously know motorcycles are close to my heart. So, if at all you are who you claim to be, we will meet next Friday at the football ground at eight in the evening. And then I will know if all this is for real. Now, we're leaving,' Koman said and beckoned Gopi to follow him.

4

I reached the football ground on the appointed day a good two hours earlier than I had been asked to. The football field, a patch of agricultural land which belonged to the Southern Railway, ran parallel to a metre-gauge railway track. On Tuesdays and Saturdays, a goods train would pass by the field at seven sharp, its high-pitched whistle rising high and hard above its steam-powered mechanical clatter. The steam engine's whistle signalled full time to the evening's matches, and I often saw the pace of a game picking up and goals being scored just as the train exited Keezhachira, where the nondescript Kollengode station was located, and rolled along the paddy fields towards Palakkad.

Usually, I'd tarry a bit at the field and watch a game or two. Some of those kids were pretty good, and you could see why Kerala was – and still is – such a powerhouse in Indian football. But that day I wanted to drive all those fuckers out of the field, especially when they lingered after their game ended, chattering about movie stars and their teachers at school and taking good-natured digs at each other. I was relieved when they finally went away, leaving me all alone in the impending darkness.

For the first time in forever, I had something to look forward to, and I anxiously hoped that the two men, one an atheist and the other a believer, would keep their word. I'm not sure why I'm telling you all this, but I was also especially glad that my attempt to take my own life centuries ago had come to naught. In the November of 1583, after a particularly nasty bout of depression, I tried to kill myself.

I travelled up the Malabar coast to the once great port city of Calicut and boarded a Portuguese ship bound for Lisbon. I don't remember much about the journey, but on a stormy night off the Cape of Good Hope, I climbed the high prow of the wooden ship, stared at the roiling ocean below me and leapt into it. But what I had longed for didn't happen. In fact, nothing happened at all. In the morning, just as I had feared, I was simply there, as I have always been.

And each time I think of that night, I'm acutely

aware that this insanity I've been infected with is the only shot I have to make my endless days more bearable.

Anyway, about twenty minutes later, I heard a motorcycle approach the field. It was the Dominator, piloted by Koman, and Gopi was sitting behind him. I ran towards them as Koman parked the motorcycle in the centre of the ground. He was wearing his trousers, instead of the mundu he usually sported after office hours, and was probably coming straight from Palakkad. Gopi was carrying a kerosene lamp, and his forehead bore religious markings – a sign of his reinforced piousness.

'I'm here, to your right,' I said.

'A-ha, ha, ha! So, you really exist?' Koman said. He looked bemused.

'Well, I'm not sure about that, but right now, I'm here.' Both of us laughed, but Gopi refused to acknowledge the joke.

'Koma, you can't make fun of everything, okay?' he said.

'All this while I thought this was a joke . . . are you sure you want to do this?' Koman asked me.

'Yes, Koma,' I said. 'I want to learn to ride like you do.'

Koman chuckled to himself. He shrugged his

shoulders, directed Gopi to fire up the lantern, and proceeded to teach me the fundamentals of motorcycling by the lantern's ghoulish glow.

Nothing I did in those first few weeks suggested that one day I would indeed be able to ride a motorcycle on my own. I stalled the Dommie many times, despaired over the lack of coordination between my feet and my hands, and had it not been for Gopi, who was always around to help me keep the motorcycle upright, the Dommie would have been riddled with scratches, dings and a lot worse.

I finally got my act together on the third weekend, when I rode without any assistance for over fifteen metres. I was definitely a bit jerky, but it was a massive leap, like a fucking Cambrian explosion, as far as my evolution as a rider went. The next milestone was a full circle of the football ground at, if I remember right, a fairly rapid pace. Then, as I turned the motorbike around to ride towards Koman and get an evaluation of my progress, he asked me to lead the Dommie out on to the road.

'Go, go, go!' he said. 'Keep going! Go all the way to the palace and come back.'

Gopi, who was right behind the bike, looked concerned, but Koman's faith in me buoyed my confidence. I took off. My right foot coaxed the clunky gears to fall into place and my right wrist modulated my advance, and the Dommie sounded wonderful as I hit the higher gears on the smooth road that led to the raja's palace. I shed a bit of speed when the first loopy bend in the road approached. I tilted my hip and leaned low along with the bike. We hugged the road and then resurrected ourselves with a flourish around the bend.

I realized, many, many years after that momentous night, that learning to ride – and eventually being consumed by motorcycling – made me feel less lonely. After years and years of being, for all practical purposes, cursedly singular, I finally had – and still have – something in common with men and women, both closer home, like Koman, and far afield. Our garages might mostly be modest affairs, but our imagination is packed with splendid motorcycles and fucking stained with grease. Our ears cock up each time a nicely noisy motorcycle passes by, and we endure the dull agony of existence because we know that soon we will ride.

Gopi leapt for joy when he saw me making my way back into the football ground.

'There he is! Kandakarnan Swamy!' he said.

I heard someone whistle – it was Koman. I looked around and was glad that nobody had seen the bike ride into the village and back. An unmanned bike, its headlight glaring ferociously, would have freaked my little village out. I was especially glad that none of those men or women were there to witness this raucous – and far-out – celebration: two men applauding and wolf-whistling at an unmanned motorcycle rushing towards them.

I killed the bike's engine and thanked Koman.

'Wonderful! I think you'll do well now, you've got the basics right,' he told me.

'Swamy, you were brilliant,' Gopi said. 'Even I wouldn't have been able to ride as smoothly as you did today.' His head was bowed and his hands were joined as always.

Koman said the best thing was that I had shifted through the gears at the right time. He had been keenly listening to the exhaust note.

'It was near perfect,' Koman said. He simultaneously made a move to slap my shoulder, but then realizing the ridiculousness of it, withdrew his commendatory gesture.

'Can I practise again next week?' I asked Koman. 'Just a couple of more times?'

'Sure, why not?'

'And . . . I hope . . . this will remain between the three of us?'

'Kandakarna, we love a good session of gossip, but a god wanting to learn how to ride? Who'd believe us!' Koman and I laughed hard and long, and this time even Gopi joined us, as heat radiated from the Dominator's pipes.

5

The Dominator left us barely months after I learnt how to ride, and I was shattered by its departure back to England with the sahib. In an effort to cheer me up, Koman gave me a bunch of motorcycle magazines, mostly British, and then, realizing that reading about bikes made me pine harder for them, he asked me to visit a big city like Coimbatore and check out the scene there. It would be a good education, he told me, and it certainly was.

On Coimbatore's broad roads, I saw motorcycles I'd never seen before and spent several Sundays at the Sulur Aerodrome, where the city's brash textile barons raced their loud, souped-up cars and bikes.

One day, on a whim, I caught a train to Madras, and decided on the way that I'd spend time at the Royal Enfield factory in Tiruvottiyur to further my understanding of the mechanics of a motorcycle. Koman had already taught me a fair deal, but I wanted to be able to take apart and put together a bike blindfolded and be this cool grease monkey who could gauge the amount of carbon deposits on a piston crown by merely listening to a motorcycle's exhaust note, or discern something graver by cocking his head towards the clatter of valves inside an engine.

I arrived in Madras on a balmy morning, and after spending many days at the city's many motorcycle showrooms and purchasing bikes vicariously through the several, mostly young, customers who sauntered in, I headed to the Royal Enfield factory. I would spend many clammy months there learning about the types of threads on fasteners, lash between gears and rubber carburettor intake hoses, about wheels within wheels and little worlds inside large ones. I won't bore you to death by going into the details of the extent of insight I acquired about motorcycles, but let's just say I was rather proud of my accomplishments and couldn't wait to head back to Kollengode and talk like an equal with Koman. Plus, there was the all-important bit about riding more, which only Koman could help me with. I had to, in racing parlance, put in more laps, and that is how I found myself in Kollengode once again.

I arrived in Kollengode at about seven in the evening and found the place uncharacteristically quiet. Usually, there would be people, especially men milling about the temples or tea shops, and Big Bazaar would just be beginning to wind down for the night. But that night, Big Bazaar had almost shut, and people around me were hurrying home. I espied Gopi at a grocer's and proceeded to project my voice in his head (you essentially hear a voice in your head; I don't really use it because it freaks people out).

Gopi and I met at a secluded spot further down from the market.

'Swamy!' He assumed a pose of supplication and told me that he was just back from a Communist Party of India meeting. Communism was all the rage back then in Kerala, and while I thought it had its merits – until it devolved into totalitarianism – it got a little trying when everybody around me talked as if they had just breakfasted with Marx and Engels.

'Welcome back, Swamy. I thought you probably got yourself a good bike and rode all the way to the heavens.'

Gopi, I always thought, was a lot more comfortable talking to me once he leapt, like a performing dog, through the hoop of piety. I found this servility highly unbecoming, especially of a communist, and never lost an opportunity to point out how he and others like him blithely reconciled religion and communism.

'I'm not that good a rider yet, comrade,' I said, and then asked about Koman and his whereabouts.

'Don't talk to me about him, Swamy. He is an idiot! I apologize to you on his behalf.'

But what had he done? Gopi couldn't bring himself to fill me in on the details of Koman's 'grave misdemeanour'. Instead, he requested me to head to Mudaliar Kulam where, he said, I would meet Koman and his great 'drama actor' friend. I was intrigued by the sudden turn of events on that dark night and raced towards Mudaliar Kulam. Upon reaching there, I saw Koman sitting on the banks of the lake. He was chatting furtively with a man who appeared to be some sort of mendicant.

'You were really good today, Rajendra! How many times do I have to tell you that you are a special talent.'

'Okay, okay, thank you, Koman Kutty sir. I've always been a little unsure . . . this is the first time I'm doing something like this.'

'No, you are good. Unlike this Prem Nazir and all these stupid film actors, you don't overact,' Koman said.

The man nodded and smiled, if a bit weakly, and thanked Koman again. He was a short man, with delicate manners, and there was a certain jumpiness about him.

'Okay, now I'm off for dinner,' Koman said. 'I'll get you some food from home, and then we will discuss the new idols and the Maha Kandarkarna puja. I really hope these bastards pay up.'

I waited until Koman was out of earshot of the man, before announcing my presence and, almost simultaneously, my perplexity.

'Hello, Koma, just what the hell is happening, da?'

Koman looked around cautiously, and then burst out laughing.

'Good you are here. Just what I wanted. Now everything will fall into place.' Before I could ask what that bloody 'everything' was, he wanted to know how my trip had been.

'Wait, wait, wait, it was all good, but it has been insinuated that you are up to something blasphemous.'

'I see you have met that idiot Gopi. Anyway, come, I'll tell you all about it. But first and most importantly, we are consecrating some new idols of you tomorrow, and I want you to be around. Now that you are here, I'll have to tweak my plan a bit–'

'My dear Koma, what is this plan and what is it for?'

A fortnight before I'd arrived, Koman had orchestrated a sequence of events that had made

Kollengode shit its pants, and he hoped it would eventually end with him having enough money to buy a motorcycle, if not a new one, at least a used bike.

The bastard had, along with Thekkepadath's Jagadeeshan, a highly unsavoury, perennially stoned character, disfigured my idols that were installed in the courtyards of his own house as well as at the Meleth and Ambat houses. And then just days later, Meleth house's Shankaran and Koman's younger brother Sethu had, in accordance with their great leader Koman's wishes, feigned severe illness. They also told their worried parents about them having recurring dreams of Kandakarnan Swamy weeping silently in a corner of Kollengode.

The air hung heavy with hushed whispers, unsolicited advice was proffered, and the piousness of the families was called into question. That was when one evening a mendicant named Vamana Panicker arrived at the village unannounced. He called for the village elders – a bunch of fat Brahmins who nervously fiddled with the sacred thread around their chests, some hirsute and pompous Nairs and Menons, and the raja – and told them that he had picked up some disturbing psychic vibrations around the village. Had something untoward occurred recently? He was on his way to the Himalayas from Kanyakumari, but he was willing to stay back and help. Vamana Panicker spoke crisp English, and when he did that it sounded like he was firing bullets from his mouth. The elders, especially the raja, were taken in by Vamana Panicker's stentorian voice and the way he struck the ground forcefully with his stick each time he wanted to emphasize a point. They also found his grasp of metaphysics and philosophy and his knowledge of the Vedas impressive, and his offer of help was accepted.

'Don't tell me this is the whiny guy you were just talking to?' I said.

'Yes and no,' said Koman, and started laughing.

He was right in a way. Vamana Panicker was not a mendicant; he was, in fact, an out-of-work actor named C. Rajendran. Rajendran had been unemployed for ages, and with good reason: while he spouted Ibsen and Shakespeare, he was hammier than Peter Ustinov, and too hammy even for the region's drama troupes that produced maudlin plays. Koman had befriended him in Palakkad and impressed by Rajendran's sincerity towards theatre, if not his acting skills, he had found him a job as a waiter at a restaurant. Rajendran was only too happy when the time came for him to repay his debt to Koman. I might have seen very little of him, but I still can't believe Kollengode fell for that twat.

Lakshmi Kutty, that morbidly obese, attention-seeking old hag from Karthedath house, fainted on seeing him; Kesavan Nair, a fervent believer in astrology, sought him out to understand if his lame thirty-five-year-old daughter would ever get married, and there were several others who claimed to have seen a fucking halo around his head. So, when after two nights of meditation by the banks of the Mudaliar Kulam Rajendran announced, I suppose, with excruciating gravitas, that an Odiyan was on the loose in Kollengode and about to wreak havoc, my people took it as gospel. An Odiyan is this feral, preternatural spirit supposedly created by sorcerers in Kerala to help you screw your enemies, and while I haven't come across him in all these years, the fucker could say the same thing about me.

'You should have seen our man that day,' Koman told me, and proceeded to give a demonstration of his friend's performance. '"What have you done to a god who guarded your village all these years?" he said. "Your apathy and your indifference towards him have rendered him so weak he cannot fight the demons who have besieged this village! I don't find it surprising that so many of you are falling sick, but soon you will all start dying. Have you people forgotten that this prosperous village has many enemies? I smell black magic, but there is a remedy."'

Rajendran proposed an urgent consecration of new idols of mine at the Azhakappadath, Meleth and Ambat houses, and a Maha Kandakarna puja to help me regain my powers and rid the village of the pestilence. Kollengode is full of misers, but the eeriness cast by the incidents of the past week did the trick. The elders decided that a donation drive would be held across the village, and the money it netted would be used to perform the puja as well as pay Rajendran a tidy token representing the village's gratitude. Koman, who was among the very few men who kept vigil around the village along with Inspector Kuriakose and his constables and had also said the right things at the right time, was asked to handle the donation drive. The drive had netted Koman a serious sum, but he estimated that he would require a little more cash to buy a used motorcycle after he had got the idols consecrated and paid for the puja and the accompanying feast.

'Rajendran has said he won't take a naya paisa from me for his help, so that money is there. I'll keep fudging, but another two hundred rupees and we will be able to pick up this beauty that's up for sale in Mannarkkad – near-mint condition 1960 model Bullet, TMV 4721–'

'Adda paavi! That's amazing, Koma, you didn't tell me about this . . . but how will you manage to get the rest of the money?' I said, and asked him what I was supposed to do.

Koman told me that he needed something dramatic to happen – like me crying – to ensure that some more money made its way into his kitty.

'Tomorrow, just before your idols are consecrated, I want you to cry and keep crying until I tell you to stop.'

I protested vigorously and told him that while his plan was fantastic on the whole, I found the bit about my crying ludicrous and a little embarrassing.

'All I'm asking you to do is to cry, or sob, or sniffle. Make yourself useful. Just what have you done in the last 10,000 years? Do you want to ride or not? Do you want us to have our own bike or not?'

I ignored the first of Koman's questions and, the next day, did as he had directed me to.

The new idols were first consecrated at the Meleth and Ambat houses early the next morning, and then we proceeded towards Azhakappadath house for the final consecration. A special ritual observance was supposed to be conducted at Azhakappadath, since it was the place where the scourge had first manifested itself. Nearly all of Kollengode had gathered at Azhakappadath house. I saw many pairs of beady eyes – especially those of Venu Nair, Kumaran Pillai and Swaminathan – intently watch a priest from one of the village's temples, as he prepared to replace the disfigured idol with the newly commissioned one.

Rajendran was seated in front of the platform that held the disfigured idol. He prayed for about a minute, and then addressed the gathering.

'Deep inside my bones, I know that Kandakarnan Swamy is weak and shrivelled up. He does not appear to have any strength left in him. I haven't been feeling any psychic vibrations!'

Koman stepped forward. 'We are consecrating the idol, Vamana Panicker sir, and, hopefully, the puja should–'

'The Maha Kandakarna puja has to happen! Otherwise this benevolent god will leave Kollengode!' Rajendran said.

There were horrified murmurs all around. Rajendran barked at everyone to be silent. He said that he intended to communicate with me, and then sat before my disfigured idol and closed his eyes.

'Vamana Panicker sir, what's happening? What is wrong?' said Koman.

'You mean you can't hear the almighty crying?'

'I . . . I'm sorry but–'

'Look at what you've done to him. Can't you people hear him cry?!'

That was my cue. I had to start crying. None of Koman's co-conspirators, including Rajendran, were aware of this particular bluff of my aural cameo.

Apart from my obvious resistance to it, I had thought it to be too bold a gambit. But Koman would have none of it.

'Kandakarna, this village, and that includes my boys, will buy exactly such irrational nonsense. I'm certain about that.'

Koman's response both confused and annoyed me. Admittedly, it was a bit rich and hypocritical of him to deny the existence of god, and then enlist the very same entity into playing a crucial part in his devious plan. But then I thought about the bike. I wanted it as badly as Koman did.

'But how does one cry without a reason?'

'I don't know, just cry. You keep telling me how sad your life is. Think about that and cry.'

So, standing next to my idol on that steamy morning, that is exactly what I did – reflect on the freakish spectacle I had turned into. I was apprehensive about whether I'd actually be able to turn on the tap. But it didn't take too long for me to become highly sentimental. At one point, I was feeling so sorry for myself that I was worried about whether I would be able to stop crying.

My plangent moans evoked a kind of horrified disbelief, and a couple of people scampered out of Azhakappadath house. Koman acted quickly. A little before the inchoate expression of my sorrows crested, he prostrated in front of my disfigured idol and begged for forgiveness. The rest of the terrified herd, including Rajendran, followed suit. I stood there, among them, reining in my grief, as my blind followers looked elsewhere. Eventually, the naked display of my vulnerabilities got a bit too embarrassing for me, and I ran out of the house and headed to Fort Maidan in Palakkad, where I spent the rest of the day staring at the sky.

On returning that evening, I encountered an upbeat Koman. He informed me that my hysterics had prompted a surge in piety – and generosity as well – among the people of Kollengode, and that he had netted way more money than he had expected to in the first place.

'Everybody's fallen for it, including our boys, and even I've had to act all spooked,' he said and laughed. The Maha Kandakarna puja was scheduled to be held in a couple of days, he said, and added rather mischievously that he expected me to be there. I skipped the puja as well as the grand farewell given to Vamana Panicker – no one ever heard of the mysterious mendicant again – and instead travelled to Coimbatore to check out the TMV 4721. I instantly took a liking to the bike. It was missing a rear foot peg, the tyres appeared scuffed and there was a crack on the headlight housing, but its engine bore no signs of that old Bullet bugbear – oil leaks – and I was happy to note that it responded with a loud roar on the very first kick each time its owner, a rotund Tamilian, straddled it.

A week later, after he'd paid off the other scamsters and settled the accounts, Koman and I journeyed together to Coimbatore to get our motorcycle home. We would eventually go on to acquire two more motorcycles that are classics today, a Jawa 250 Type 353 and a 1986 Yamaha RD350, and while both were absolute peaches in their own ways, the scruffy TMV 4721 was what made me the rider I am today. And I'd like to think I'm pretty good. Maybe not world level like Valentino Rossi, or that crazy motherfucker Kevin Schwantz, but, all other things being equal, on a winding road I could whip your sorry ass and hand it to you.

6

In the late 1960s, I left for England to check out the motorcycling scene there. I had won Koman's respect and admiration for the rapidity with which I had evolved into a skilful rider. He called me a 'natural', and that made me very happy. After we had completed a really long blast down south from Hyderabad to Kanyakumari – Koman would mock-grip the handlebars while I rode – he decided that I was now ready for sterner but more exciting tests.

I was in two minds initially, but finally succumbed to Koman's unceasing insistence and the promise of a world with motorcycles more powerful, faster and more beautiful than any I'd ridden before. Besides, as Koman said, who would have missed me in Kollengode anyway.

England was a revelation. What a summer that was. The Beatles. Flower power. And thousands of magnificent motorcycles glinting in the golden sun. And the tone and timbre of their exhaust notes – rorty, sibilant, gravelly, growly, snarly, and gloriously raw and unapologetically loud. Brough Superiors, Triumph Speed Twins, Tigers, Thunderbirds and T120 Bonnevilles, Velocette Venoms, cafe racers of all kinds, Ducatis, Gileras, and even a 1950 Norton Manx. I made my pilgrimages in England. I first went to Triumph's facility in Coventry and then to Birmingham, where the factories of BSA and Velocette were located, and after checking out Royal Enfield's plant at Redditch, I landed in Wolverhampton, where I mourned the closure of that great marque Sunbeam. Then I started homing in on my targets.

The first motorcycle I rode in Britain was an Ariel Red Hunter, borrowed, without permission of course, from a neat little home in Tunbridge Wells. For obvious reasons, I always rode at night and rode fast – it was tough, even in 1960s' England, to ride unnoticed – and I had to jettison way more machines than I swung a leg over. A Matchless Silver Streak (beautiful close-ratio gearbox!), near Hastings; an unbelievably smooth Velocette Venom, along the Antrim Coast; a Panther Model 100, near Inverness;

and a BSA Rocket Goldstar, near Tenterden, were some of the other magnificent motorcycles that provided me with intense rushes of joy.

But my eagerness to ride almost got me arrested. After my nineteenth jaunt, on a smooth but bulky Ariel Square Four, whose progress was frequently impeded by overheating problems, I felt like having a go at the Isle of Man circuit. I thought I'd travel to the island, filch a nice Norton International, or a Triton, from one of the kids out there, and do a quick lap on that hallowed street circuit, but a news item in the *Daily Mirror* dissuaded me from embarking on that adventure. The report, headlined 'Mysterious but honourable motorcycle thief on the prowl', spoke about a rider who mooched fast motorcycles after sundown, rode them hard, and mostly left them unblemished by the side of the road, often not too far from where they had been stolen. Over the last two months, the mysterious rider, the report said, had struck in many places as far afield as Sunderland and Brighton.

A pattern had emerged after the police in different counties spoke with each other, and the consensus, arrived at after observing the worn-out foot pegs and scuffed tyres, was that the man they were looking for was a highly skilled motorcyclist with a fine taste in motorcycles. A police official from London said that it was an 'exceedingly queer case, but we have a few leads and we should be able to track him down'.

I felt chuffed when I chanced upon the report, but I also saw it as a sign to lie low for a bit, at least in England. So I travelled to Munich to visit BMW's motorcycle factory, and a day later, crossed over to Italy where I couldn't keep my hands off some more motorbikes, among them a Ducati 250 Mach1 – fast, stylish and very uncompromising – a Gilera Saturno and a brutish Moto Guzzi V7 750 Special, which had these slanting cylinder heads peeping out of its frame. The ride on the Moto Guzzi marked the end of my first proper trip abroad.

I considered going to Japan and the United States but didn't feel particularly excited at the thought of riding Harley-Davidsons, or any of the new Hondas or Kawasakis. I could do all of that later, I told myself, and, nudged by sudden pangs of homesickness, headed back home.

On reaching Kollengode, I immediately travelled with Gopi to Palakkad. We met Koman there and the two friends finished two bottles of Cutty Sark whisky, as I enthralled them at the Fort Maidan late into the night narrating tales of my trysts with all those exotic machines. Over the years, I have visited many countries in search of interesting motorcycles and ridden a million mooched miles on all sorts of machines. Each of these adventures helped Koman vicariously live the thrill of riding motorcycles he had never had the opportunity to ride.

But there is a story that was better than all my stories. It is about the Velocette Venom Thruxton HT, and the man who narrated it to us, on a September night, was Kadar.

The boys were all at the arrack shop celebrating Koman's engagement to Achath house's Madhavi, which had taken place earlier that day. An exuberant Koman had ordered meat of various kinds – frog's legs, beef, fowl and mutton – to go with the several litres of alcohol that he and his band of merrymakers consumed that night.

Much advice was proffered by some of Koman's married friends, especially Murthy, the twice-divorced rascal, who distilled his bitter wisdom for the soon-to-be groom's benefit. Koman and his friends talked about the football games they had played as children, the various teachers they had harassed, cursed CK and Gopalan for not being around, and wondered why Gopi was still unmarried.

'Must be because of that girl he desired so much. Koma, what was her name? The one who used to pass this way daily on the bus to Nemmara?' asked Choochai Narayanan, a wave of mirth cresting on his grandly moustachioed face.

'Savitri . . . Savitri Kutty,' Koman bellowed.

'But wasn't she from a rich family? I heard her father was a contractor . . . they have two cars, I think,' said Velayudhan, who had studied with Koman until class eight and now worked as a bus conductor.

'Was one of the cars an Impala?' asked Koman, who, after taking another swig from his glass, flashed a knowing smile at Gopi.

As if on cue, the other revellers broke into a popular Malayalam song which, roughly translated, starts off on this bitter note:

'Oh, I'm just a poor Morris Minor,
She was a '71 Impala . . .'

Every line in the song, accompanied by the off-key drumming of fingers and banging of fists on the wooden tables, was followed by roars of laughter. To be frank, while I had accompanied the bunch to the arrack shop, I felt a little vague about the whole thing. I was happy for Koman, but I always pictured him dramatically eloping with someone, possibly from another religion or caste, rather than willingly submitting to the mundane ubiquitousness of an arranged marriage. On the other hand, it would also be accurate to say that I felt a bit possessive about him. Of course, Madhavi was a sweet woman with big eyes and the talk was that she was an excellent cook, but I was apprehensive of things being never quite the same again between us. We were an unlikely duo but we got along pretty well, thanks to motorcycles, and I hoped he would still be around to share my rabid enthusiasm for bikes, and lend a patient ear to my singular woes even if he made light of them.

'The point is they are not there. Your worries, sorrows, they don't exist,' he said.

'How is that?'

'Because you don't.'

And sometimes, I think I should swallow that placebo for my perennial affliction.

Kadar arrived just as the party was about to end, and a sentimental Koman decided to drink yet another glass as a tribute to the man who had taught him everything he knew about motorbikes.

'This is the one man who has never judged Koman Kutty,' he said, as if he was addressing a gathering, and, on realizing that the only people left in the shop were Gopi and Balan, the owner, he sought the latter's ear.

'Listen Balaetta, come sit here. This man, this Kadar bhai, didn't care about what I drank, or where I slept during all those years I roamed like a vagabond. He shared his knowledge with me,' said Koman, gesturing towards Kadar.

'You want to know about motorcycles, you go to him. What are you riding these days, Kadar bhai?'

'Nothing special, a Lambretta that's come in for repair,' said Kadar, who wore a highly amused expression and was probably thinking about the hundreds of times he had seen Koman in a similar state.

'KHU 8765? Two-tone colour – blue and white? Aaaaanh! I saw you last week on it.'

When the conversation started revolving around motorcycles, I got up from the table at the farthest end of the arrack shop and sat right beside Koman. Under the yellowish glare of a swaying 60 watt lamp, the mentor and his protégé spoke about motorcycles launched abroad that year or thereabouts – the Yamaha RD350, the Honda CB400F, the four-cylinder CB750 and the MV Agusta 750 Sport. They rued, yet again, the end of the British motorcycle industry. But Koman still held the hope that Triumph would somehow manage to turn it around.

'No, they are hopelessly out of touch with the

times. Look at the Japanese bikes, you ride them for thousands of kilometres and nothing goes wrong. But once a British bike starts acting up, not even Allah can save you.'

'But Kadaretta, once they get going, it's adipoli! I don't think any Japanese motorcycle, all this Kawasaki-wawasaki can match our good old British motorcycles . . . Kadaretta, promise me if you ever decide to part with your bikes, I'll be informed of it first.'

'Of course, Koma, but it is not time yet. My rides on my motorcycles are the only thing I look forward to.'

'But Kadaretta, promise me that you will? Aaanh. Appo, I have this . . . this friend who regularly goes to London and Europe and gets to ride all these new motorcycles,' said Koman, obliquely referring to me.

'He . . . deals in spare parts in Madras and Bombay, and he recently rode a Norton Yellow Peril.'

'A Yellow Peril? Appa, that's the Norton Commando Production Racer. It has high compression pistons, a gas-flowed head and a racing camshaft. Lucky rascal.'

'Super thing, apparently.'

'Who is this friend? How does he get to ride all these motorcycles? I have to meet him. You said he deals in spare parts?'

'Yes. In a way. His father is a big man at Premier,

you know, Fiats, and this guy is also interested in motorcycles. So, each time he goes abroad, he spends time in Europe-kerope, riding all these motorcycles. He fell in love with British bikes while studying in London. He comes from money.'

Kadar nodded. 'Next time you see him, ask him if he has ever heard of a motorcycle called the Thruxton HT . . . Velocette Venom Thruxton HT.'

Both Koman and I were big Velocette fans. I had even ridden a Velo, but hadn't as yet managed to get my hands on a Thruxton. But the HT?

'Yes, I, too, have enquired with many people, but nobody has heard of this particular motorcycle. If it exists then I think it could be the world's greatest motorcycle.'

'How is that?' asked Koman, leaning towards Kadar.

'Come, you've had enough. Let's go out and get some fresh air.'

The four of us trooped out. Outside, a cool breeze that still smelled of rain wicked away the beads of perspiration on Koman's and Gopi's faces, and a bunch of palm civets feasted noisily atop a mango tree. Kadar sat sideways on his parked Lambretta, while his two friends crowded around him.

'Shaiii! Move! You people stink!'

'Aaaah, that's okay, tell me about this motorcycle,' said Koman, unmindful of the teetotaller Kadar's obvious discomfort.

'Appo, about two years ago, one of my spare parts dealer friends in Coimbatore wrote to me saying that he had referred my name to two men who were on their way to Kerala from Allahabad,' said Kadar. 'He said that they wanted help with a particular motorcycle. They believed the motorcycle was in Kerala. He requested me to provide every possible assistance to the two men who were expected to arrive soon. I wrote back saying I would.'

7

Back in the 1960s, if you owned any sort of proper vehicle in Allahabad, you would probably have been a customer of Singh & San's Auto Spares. It was said that Gurjit Singh and his Chinese wife, Ng Swee San, who ran the store, even supplied spare parts for some of the then Prime Minister Jawaharlal Nehru's official cars. The couple had migrated from Lahore after Partition, along with Gurjit's mother Charanjit Kaur, and had two kids. Peter, the elder, was quiet and studious. But his chubby brother, Chowfin, younger by two years and with a curious birthmark – nine moles ringing his belly button – was supposed to be a speed demon, who as a child would keep pestering his father to take him along on motorcycle rides. By the time he turned fifteen, Chowfin was already sneaking rides in Gurjit's Chrysler Airflow and on his BSA Bantam.

Gurjit decided to groom Peter to take over his business as the boys tumbled out of their teens; Chowfin, he hoped, would eventually come to his senses and do something other than ride, drive and mess with engines all day. He had no aptitude for business, and no amount of reprimands from either of his parents stopped him from riding and driving scarily fast.

Eventually, Gurjit acted on the advice of his mother, Charanjit, who doted on Chowfin, and, leveraging his goodwill with his spare parts suppliers abroad, sent him to England to work as an apprentice with the British car company Jaguar. But, within three months of his departure, Chowfin told his father that he would ideally want to work for a motorcycle company. So, Gurjit worked through his contacts once again, and, in 1968, Chowfin Singh was at work in Velocette Motorcycles' red-brick building at Hall Green in Birmingham. Chowfin and his family stayed in touch through letters and the odd phone call. The job didn't pay much, but Chowfin told his parents and brother that he was the happiest he'd ever been helping put together those gleaming machines, one of which he hoped, if his father were to chip in with some cash, to buy very soon. He had also spoken to his superiors about being part of Velocette's racing team as a member of the support staff, and thought he had a real chance of getting in. Towards the end of Chowfin's second year in England, Peter received a letter from his brother that conveyed both joy and concern in equal measure. Chowfin had been chosen to join Velocette's racing team and accompany them for a few local races, but he was also worried about rumours of Velocette shutting down. Apart from the Venom and the Thruxton, they had mostly produced lemons in the 1960s. Chowfin said that if Velocette went belly-up, he would try his luck at Triumph, or if all else failed, come back to India and work for Royal Enfield. But he was also hopeful of Velocette fighting back. He had heard that the company was building another motorcycle – a 750cc – and a lot was expected of it. Very few people had seen the motorcycle prototype – it was top secret – but Chowfin promised Peter that he would write to him as soon as he got to see it. That was the last his family heard from him. About a year later, Peter's search for his missing brother led him inexplicably to Kollengode.

When Kadar met Peter, a courteous young man with prominent ears, and his interpreter, a man from Kottayam called Raman, at their room at Ambili Lodge in Kollengode, Peter told him that it was a series of recurring dreams that had brought him to Kerala.

'I'd dream of Chowfin riding this motorbike along the sea, the coconut groves, canals, little villages exactly like this one, you know, with the tea stalls and the temples . . . I knew it had to be Kerala, which is why I'm here,' said Peter. 'At one level it doesn't make any sense; nothing that I'm going to tell you will really make sense. But I stopped having those dreams as soon as we entered Kerala.'

Peter and Raman had journeyed up the coast from Trivandrum, and spoken to several people, especially mechanics and petrol pump owners, but had drawn a blank.

'Peter sir wrote back to Chowfin and the family waited, but there was no response. Then they heard that Velocette was shutting down and immediately called up Chowfin's landlady, who said that it had been weeks since she had seen him. And so, Peter sir and his father left for England,' Raman told Kadar.

Despite making several enquiries with Chowfin's former colleagues and his landlady, who handed over Chowfin's belongings to them, Peter and Gurjit found themselves at a dead end a week after they arrived in Birmingham. They registered a missing persons case with the police, put out advertisements that promised a handsome reward in return for information on Chowfin in a few local newspapers, and waited for the phone to ring. Four days later, they got a call at their hotel. The hoarse voice at the other end introduced himself to Peter as Jaroslav Vesely. Vesely, who spoke English tentatively, said he had information on Chowfin and asked them to meet him later that day at Victoria Park.

Jaroslav Vesely was an empty shell of a man, with the look of someone who had witnessed something wondrously terrifying. Peter said there was no life in his eyes. On that chilly evening at the park, Vesely said that he and Chowfin had travelled with the Velocette racing team or whatever was left of it to a couple of local races before the company began winding down its operation. He had hit it off with Chowfin since he had also worked with Jawa at its factory in Mysore and its dealerships in Bombay and Delhi in the early 1960s.

'All of what I'm going to tell you now actually happened. Please believe me,' Vesely said.

In the first week of November 1970, Vesely and Chowfin, who were back at work in the factory after Velocette disbanded its racing team, were asked to report early one morning at the company's test track. On reaching there, in the backdrop of a loud rumble, they saw the company's owner Bertie Goodman ('BJG') and four other important-looking men follow the rapid progress of a motorcycle on the test track. It was a cold morning that smelled of strong cologne and cigarettes and gasoline.

'Gentlemen, the Velocette Venom Thruxton HT. It's a big gamble, but I'm certain it will pay off. In a couple of months, we should be back on track,' said Goodman, as the test rider brought the motorcycle to a halt a couple of metres from where the group was standing. The important-looking men nodded tentatively. Some coffee was unflasked, and Vesely and Chowfin were asked to do a quick check of the mechanicals before one of the other test riders had a go at the HT.

'I remember Chowfin nudged me when we walked towards it. He was very excited. So was I. But we were not happy when we got closer to the motorcycle. It didn't look very different from the regular Thruxton, except for one thing – it had a huge engine. Four cylinders, inline. I thought it was too large for that bike, and I'm sure it would have affected the riding dynamics. It looked very odd to me. No one would have bought a motorcycle like that,' said Vesely.

Vesely called out to the next test rider after the motorcycle had been given a once-over, and the man started walking towards the bike.

'That was when the bike snarled, Mr Peter. It really snarled.'

Chowfin and Vesely hastily moved away from the motorcycle, their bosses turned around, and the rider froze. An eerie creek slithered through the air, as the bike eased itself off the central stand and advanced towards the test rider.

'Then it leapt ahead and knocked him down hard. Just like that, Mr Singh, just like that. And after that, it charged at our bosses.'

People scattered; the big bosses backed away towards the gates of the track, but BJG ordered Chowfin and Vesely to find a safe place and stay put at the track while they fetched the cops.

The test rider's compatriot was a brave man. He rushed to his fallen comrade, but just as he was about to lift the unconscious man off the ground, the motorcycle turned around and rammed into him. Vesely ran towards the makeshift grandstand and shouted out to Chowfin to do the same.

'But he just stood there. I remember him saying, "JV sir, I'm going to have some fun."'

There were a couple of things he remembered, Vesely told the Singhs. He remembered vociferously and repeatedly ordering Chowfin to step back; he watched with alarm as Chowfin charged towards the HT, and he remembered his colleague and that seemingly sentient machine wrestle with each other.

The motorcycle kept trying to throw Chowfin off, but he tenaciously clung on to it, trying all the time to switch the ignition on and kick-start it. It was a violent struggle, Vesely said, and he was afraid the motorcycle would kill Chowfin.

'And then Chowfin won,' said Vesely. 'He started her up. I saw him twist the throttle like a maniac, and they disappeared down the test track.' Barely five seconds later, Vesely saw the rider and the HT again, coming at him like a bullet.

'He was very quick, quicker than anyone I've seen, and I've seen the greats, I've seen them all. I thought he'd crash at the end of the long straight if he didn't brake before the turn, but he took that corner without braking; he went through! I don't know how he did it.' Vesely said that Chowfin and the HT went around the track thrice, and then, with a murderously loud noise, the motorcycle took off with its rider.

'What?' Peter said.

'Yes, straight over my head. He waved out to me. Chowfin was laughing hard. I watched them go higher and higher until, Mr Peter, until I could no longer see them.'

Vesely got up abruptly. 'I don't want any reward if this information helps you locate him. I just hope he comes back. He was a good man,' he said, and shuffled away into the night.

Peter and his father stayed in England for a few more days, during which time they tried to get in touch with Bertie Goodman. They were told that he was away in Italy, but the Singhs managed to locate both the injured test riders. But it wasn't of much help. The two men had apparently not spoken to anyone since the incident and had the same lifeless look in their eyes as Vesely did. On the twentieth day after they had arrived in England, the distraught father and son returned to Allahabad.

'I didn't know what to say. Peter seemed like an earnest guy, but . . .' said Kadar.

He sat silent for a while. A red state transport bus whooshed by noisily, and a bullock cart crept towards us in the distance, the lashes from its driver's whip alternating with the tinkling of the bells around the neck of the draught animal. I stood still, processing the information Kadar had provided. Four cylinders? Was it a response to the legendary Honda CB750? The Japanese company had really raised the bar with that machine. But, more importantly, I quite fancied the idea of a motorcycle that chose its riders. I wondered what the Thruxton HT, if it did exist, would have been like to ride.

'Aaanh! So what happened after that?' Koman's characteristic impatience broke Kadar's reverie.

'What could have happened? I was very frank. I told him that I had never heard of a Velocette four-cylinder bike, and that by the end of the 1960s, they were in the doldrums anyway – where would they find the money to develop a new four-cylinder bike? But he was such a nice guy, so I told Peter that if his brother ever happened to swing by, and if I happened to hear of it, I would immediately write to him.'

Peter thanked Kadar profusely, and showed him the most recent photograph he had of Chowfin. It had been taken a few weeks after he started working for Velocette. 'He was a chubby, sweet-looking kid, long hair and all,' said Kadar.

Peter told Kadar that he usually never revealed the whole story about his missing brother, but he said he had a nice feeling about Kollengode.

'I know it sounds unbelievable, and I don't even have any company documents to prove that there was indeed such a running prototype. But you know, the moment we entered this village, this place felt very familiar to me. That lake, the shrines. It's as if Chowfin is somehow connected to it. And you look like you are a good man. Thank you once again, sir. Inshallah, we will speak soon.'

Koman, Gopi and Kadar listened to each other's silences for a bit, and then Gopi said, 'It all sounds so ridiculous, but would a man travel all the way from Allahabad if there wasn't anything to it? And what about those dreams? He said they stopped as soon as they reached Kerala.'

'Gopi, what nonsense are you talking about, you imbecile! Dreams, it seems. Yes, a man can go missing in England, but what about the rest? Nonsense! A motorcycle can't take off – it's against the laws of physics!'

'You are right, Koma,' said Kadar. 'But, let me tell you, a couple of months after they left I was in Coimbatore when I met the friend who had directed Peter to me. I had forgotten about Peter's visit, but apparently the whole family had died in a car accident just weeks after Peter got back to Allahabad. It all seems very strange.'

'Kadaretta, am I drunk or are you drunk?' said Koman.

Kadar smiled and kick-started his scooter. 'Who knows, Koma. But if a bike like that is out there somewhere, I'd like to ride it.'

'Bloody fools,' Koman said, and walked back inside the arrack shop. Gopi followed him inside and I heard the two friends arguing about the Thruxton HT.

Nobody asked me for my opinion, but if they had, I'd have told them the same thing: 'If it exists, I'd like to ride it.' But if it did exist and if I did get a chance to ride it, would I prove to be, as Chowfin Singh had all those years ago, its equal? I know this bit about a fat man taming a ferocious bike and taking off into the heavens sounds improbable, but, you tell me, is it as improbable as an agnostic village deity falling in love with motorcycles?

8

About two months ago, I nearly had a heart attack. I was at the S.S. Manikandan & Sons' store in Palakkad, flipping through the latest issues of automobile journals, when I came across an article by Rishabhh Mehtaa in *Turbo* magazine.

Rishabhh, *Turbo*'s peripatetic correspondent, had written about his drive from Delhi to Varanasi in a hellishly red Jaguar F-Type S convertible as well as the time he spent in the constituency of India's prime minister and number one gas bag, Narendra Modi. The crazy bugger had really gunned it and covered the distance between Allahabad and Varanasi in barely eighty minutes. The highlight of the drive for him was a pronounced kink in the road, about forty-seven kilometres from Varanasi. Our man was doing about 110 kays, and he entered the corner almost flat out!

'For a moment I thought I had carried too much speed into the turn, but that didn't stop me from exiting with my foot squashing the accelerator. The Jag loved it. Her tail twitched happily and the tyres chirped, but I dabbed in some opposite lock, caught her just as she started sliding and brought her to heel.'

The Jag's race-bred 492bhp V8 engine is supposed to be a bomb. What fun he must have had! Rishabhh Mehtaa had encountered all kinds of people at the epicentre of Hinduism: oleaginous priests who promised salvation to his forefathers, piles of garbage, Naga sadhus with 'desire rotting in their eyes', and an uncouth bunch of Modi bhakts. But the climactic moment of his journey, so to speak, came on his last day in Varanasi. He was thoroughly unprepared for it, and so was I when I reached the end of the piece.

'I hit the Grand Trunk Road early the next morning and drive towards Chunar, about thirty kilometres from Varanasi. It is not light yet, but I am in the zone. She is purring sweetly, like only a Jaguar can. I like the vibe this car gives out. It's not as quick as a Porsche 911, but with a good driver behind the wheel, it can nip at the German's heels.

'I have been to Chunar before. It's a quiet village with a fifteenth-century fort overlooking the banks of the Ganga. I drive up to the fort and take out my camera. A dusty road leads up to an embankment and, for as far as the eye can see, the Ganga flows serenely eastward. Sitting on its banks, I think of my life: my little triumphs and big disappointments, old loyalties and fresh betrayals, about how far I have come and how much farther I have to go.

'A day later, a little before sunset, I head back to the ghats of Varanasi one last time. The river is infused with a mellow light. From where I am standing on the ghats, the Ganga meanders lazily, almost coming to a standstill. The devout take dips in the water, heads and hands raised towards the heavens, while little boats carrying tourists glide by. Groups of men huddle at the feet of saffron-clad sadhus. It is a tranquil scene, though they should really do something about these goats that shit all over the place.

'Ever since I began handling the travel section of this magazine about eight years ago, I have driven to many places across the world. Some moments have made certain places more memorable than others. When I think of the Himalayas, I think of one particular stretch between Zing Zing Bar and Baralacha La that I traversed on a windy night, as the mountains cast ominous shadows all around. I often think of a resplendent early morning in Wadi Rum, in Jordan; I'll also never forget that meal of couscous and tagine chicken I had near Essaouira, in Morocco; the moss-coated palaces of Mandu on a rainy evening; and the ruins of Orchha on a cold night. Would this moment on the ghats of Varanasi prove to be as indelible, I wonder. Just then, I see a large, bare-chested man walk out of the water, up the steps that lead from the river towards the ghats. He is around sixty, but baby-faced, and with cheeks that bulge out from under his eyes. He appears to be of mixed ancestry. He has an unruly but robust moustache, and he wears his thinning silver hair long. As he makes his way up the steps, he turns towards me and waves. I am surprised, but I wave back, and my eyes fall on a peculiar birthmark that is emblazoned on his enormous belly. Encircling his belly button is an arrangement of nine moles of varying sizes. They appear to be frozen in orbit. I get up and follow him, about ten paces behind, as he makes his way out of the ghats. I see him walk towards a motorcycle parked by the side of the bustling street. It has a distinctive exhaust. A fishtail muffler! Is it a Velocette? As far as I know, there aren't too many authentic Velocettes in India.

'Under its tank, I can make out the outline of a huge engine. A four-cylinder unit? I thought Velocette mostly made single-cylinder motorcycles, apart from some dull flat twins. Plus, the engine looked rather big for the motorcycle. What is this motorcycle doing in Varanasi and who is this mysterious man? I jostle my way through the human concourse, but the man has already kick-started his motorcycle. In about two seconds, he is off. Only the sonorousness of the motorcycle's exhaust note lingers in the dusty air. A large man with a peculiar birthmark takes a bath in the Ganga and then vrooms away on a rare British bike – it couldn't have happened anywhere in the world but Varanasi. It is that kind of a place.'

I don't quite remember what happened to me after I read the concluding paragraph of Rishabhh Mehtaa's story the first time. I think I must have fainted. The elation, the adrenaline rush, and the anxiety – it was all too much. All I can recall is that sometime during the night, I revived and reread the piece innumerable times, and kept staring at it until the words dissolved into the page.

So, Kadar had been right. There really was a Velocette Venom Thruxton HT, and its rider could have been none other than Chowfin Singh. That much was incontrovertible.

The writer, though he was unaware of the actual import of who and what he had witnessed, had seen them both. Of course, there were chances that the motorcycle had been a mod job – people do all sorts of things to their bikes these days – but what do you have to say about that birthmark around his belly button?

I sat there at Manikandan's store in a fug of cloying aromas, predominantly that of overripe bananas and incense sticks, and wished Koman were around. Had he been alive and healthy – he would definitely have been more open to acknowledging the existence of the Thruxton HT after, maybe, getting in touch with Rishabhh Mehtaa – Koman would have been in his late seventies by now, but I don't think my friend would have been able to resist accompanying me on one last ride in pursuit of the world's badass-est motorcycle. We would have headed straight to Allahabad, of course. Chowfin Singh was either on his way there, or, after learning of the tragedy that had befallen his family, on his way back from Allahabad to, well, I don't know where.

Perhaps he had visited Varanasi to seek some solace, but I suppose he could have gone anywhere after that: up north towards Chandigarh, Simla and the Himalayas, or further east on the Grand Trunk Road towards Calcutta, or down south.

A man like him with a bike like that could cover a massive distance in a day, but he would have to stop to rest, to eat, to refuel. Koman and I would have had to ride out of our skin, but – unless he had blasted off into the skies – I was certain we would have eventually picked up his scent. In all probability, we would have chased Chowfin Singh on a nice Triumph or one of these lovely new Royal Enfield Interceptors. Koman had an excellent network of contacts and would have had to call in a few favours – but, ideally, my weapon of choice, though I don't really dig Japanese bikes, would have been the Kawasaki Z1.

The Kwacker, which exploded on to the scene in the early 1970s, was insanely powerful and immensely reliable, and it could fly. Just the thing to have when you are pursuing the world's best bike and the world's best rider. Or, the hopeless romantic that I am, I thought, hell, why not get a great British motorcycle to chase another one? The first superbike versus a mental monster? V-twin versus four-cylinder? The Vincent Black Shadow versus the Velocette Venom Thruxton HT: Dibdibdibddddoooowahhhhaaarr versus, I don't know, bruuuuuuuuggggghhhhhaaaaaaaaghhhh?

I would have probably sat at Manikandan's the whole night, invoking majestic beasts from the motorcycling pantheon if it were not for the dusty grandfather clock in the shop that chimed twice. It was two in the morning. There would be no Kawasaki Z1s or Vincent Black Shadows and, worst of all, there was no Koman. Chowfin Singh and the Thruxton HT rapidly receded from my overwrought imagination, and then farther and farther away until I could no longer see them. If I was to pursue them, I would need an ally. Someone who would believe in an improbable story told by an improbable narrator; a person who could squander away a lifetime in search of stirring rides. I would need another Koman.

I put the magazine back on the rack, and thought of Rishabhh Mehtaa. Wasn't he the only person in the world to have actually seen Chowfin Singh and the Thruxton HT over four decades after they mysteriously disappeared? Wasn't there something to that? It was worth a try.

I bolted out of Manikandan's and ran past Tipu Sultan's fort towards the Yakkara bridge. After a series of rides on the back of trucks heading north from Palakkad, I arrived at Kollengode's only Internet cafe, Enkay Cool Bar & Net Nest, booted up one of the two computers, and switched on the router. So, www.turbomag.com–Enter–Search 'Rishabhh Mehtaa'–Enter.

Over the last four to five years, Rishabhh Mehtaa had driven the BMW Gran Turismo, in Spain; a Mini Clubman, in Puerto Rico; and the Volvo S80, in Delhi; and ridden the Ducati Scrambler, in Goa. One of the links my query threw up led me to the Turbo Team page and what I read on it, specifically about Rishabhh Mehtaa, made me happy. Here is what I read:

> Rishabhh Mehtaa, assistant editor.
>
> Loves Chrysler Hemi engines.
>
> And 1980s' two-stroke bikes. And intelligent women and beer.
>
> Likes his steak rare.
>
> Listens to Metal, Prog-rock and rorty exhaust notes.
>
> Hates exercise and Korean cars.
>
> Fastest drive ever: 291 kph, in a Ferrari 458 Spyder, around Maranello, Italy.
>
> Favourite F1 driver: Jochen Rindt.
>
> Bucket list: Paris–Dakar, in a Tatra truck; Isle of Man TT, on a Britten V1000; and Carrera Pan Americana, in a Mercedes-Benz 300 SL 'Gullwing'.
>
> Wants to flatline with his riding boots/driving shoes on.

The snappy bio was accompanied by a photograph of a man in his early thirties: short, slightly plump, wavy hair, goatee, glares, and he was standing next to a Lamborghini Countach, that brutally significant supercar from the 1980s. Despite the extra letters in his name and that silly goatee, here, I thought, was a true enthusiast. One of us. You would find many people raving about Lamborghinis, Ferraris, Ducatis and BMW M5s, but you needed to be virulently in love with machines to actually include a Tatra truck on your automotive bucket list. But would he be the one?

I would soon find out.

9

To: editor@turbomagazine.com
Cc: rishabhhmehtaa@turbomagazine.com

Dear Sir,
I have been an avid reader of automobile magazines for a long time. I have also had the pleasure of being informed and entertained by Turbo *since its inception.*

I write to you with regard to an article headlined 'Mend in the River' by your correspondent Rishabhh Mehtaa, who is copied on this email, in your latest issue. The article was about his journey to Varanasi, and his brief sighting of a rare British motorcycle there. As he rightly deduced from the fishtail exhaust, the motorcycle could actually have been a Velocette Venom, or possibly its racetrack-oriented version, the Thruxton. The fishtail exhaust was, of course, a very Velocette design motif.

The fishtail silencer, I'm sure you would be aware, was very similar to the Brooklands silencer, so named because this sort of exhaust was first mandated for cars and bikes at the Brooklands Speed Bowl, in Great Britain, one of the very first special motor racing circuits in the world.

In his article, Mr Mehtaa wrote that he thought he discerned the outline of a four-cylinder engine under the tank of the motorcycle. This was among the things in the article that I found especially intriguing. That's because Velocette never put a four-cylinder motorcycle into production. They mostly made single-cylinder engines. However, there were reports of Velocette developing a four-cylinder engine in the 1960s. But the Thruxton HT prototype was a different beast. It was, according to some people, this mercurial, almost sentient machine with a massive engine that even the best riders at Velocette failed to tame when it was being tested. Now, however unlikely it might sound, I am wondering whether it is indeed this prototype – Velocette is said to have built only one – that Mr Mehtaa chanced upon in Varanasi.

If it is indeed the Thruxton HT, it could be a global scoop for Turbo. *I don't think any magazine has ever written about the HT, or even seen it.*

But I do have a couple of questions for Mr Mehtaa. I will be grateful if he could respond to them:

1. *Was the motorcycle Mr Mehtaa saw a mod job? I suppose one could transplant a four-cylinder engine from another motorcycle; now I wouldn't do that, but it can be done.*
2. *According to Mr Mehtaa, the rider had a very peculiar birthmark – nine moles arranged around his belly button. Could it have been that Mr Mehtaa mistook a more pedestrian birthmark for such a singular arrangement of moles?*

I apologize for the scepticism my missive appears to be sprinkled with, but it is mild in nature, and also for the tangential curiosity about the birthmark on the belly of the motorcycle's rider. But what I'm essentially seeking is a reconfirmation of a fascinating story I heard long ago about the Thruxton HT. It involved an Indian mechanic from Allahabad with the very same birthmark Mr Mehtaa mentions in his travelogue! He was, supposedly, the only man who tamed the Thruxton HT.

However, we know very little about what happened to the machine and its rider after he, I believe, blitzed a test track in Birmingham in late 1970.

With all due respect, I'm not sure if Mr Mehtaa and you are aware of this story, but I'm certain both of you are excited about the sighting of a Velocette. There are, after all, only a handful of them in India.

Should my email motivate him to delve deeper into the story behind what is, in all probability, Velocette's most fascinating creation, I would be delighted to supply him with whatever information I have on the said motorcycle and its rider. We are talking here about a magnificent machine and a supremely skilled rider the world doesn't know about and deserves to know more about.

Best,

KK Swamy

ridesaferidehard@gmail.com

~

To: ridesaferidehard@gmail.com
From: rishabhhmehtaa@turbomagazine.com

Hello Mr Swamy,
Can't wait to chat about this! However, I'm a bit tied up with closing the issue at the moment. But you are going to hear from me very soon.

Cheers,

Rishabhh Mehtaa

Assistant Editor (Features)

Turbo *Magazine*

14-24, Belle Vue Condominium

P.B. Marg, Opposite Century Mills,

Worli, Mumbai-27
O: 91222478767

~

To: rishabhhmehtaa@turbomagazine.com
From: ridesaferidehard@gmail.com

Dear Mr Mehtaa,
Thank you so much for your mail. It is a great pleasure to hear back from a fellow enthusiast. (I am seriously impressed by some of your choices which I happened to read about on your website – Favourite F1 driver: Jochen Rindt; Bucket list: Paris–Dakar, in a Tatra truck!)

Eagerly looking forward to hearing from you again, and I hope I will because time is of great essence here.

Sincerely yours,
KK Swamy

~

To: rishabhhmehtaa@turbomagazine.com
From: ridesaferidehard@gmail.com

Dear Mr Mehtaa,
Trust you are doing fine, and that the edition of Turbo *you were working on has been sent to the press.*

I look forward to continuing our discussion, and hope that we can take this forward. I fear the moment to act may soon pass.

Sincerely yours,

KK Swamy

~

Dear Mr Mehtaa,

I'd be much obliged if you could respond to my email which I sent to you and your editor three days ago. I have a very interesting proposition to make, and my gut says you will take it up.

Sincerely,

KK Swamy

~

Dear Mr Mehtaa,

I have decided to come to Mumbai and meet you. This won't be easy for either me or you, but it can't wait any more. I hope you will give me a bit of your time.

See you soon.

Sincerely yours,

KK Swamy

10

I landed at Rishabhh's place on a Friday night after plucking his address from a register at his workplace, and found him lost in a pungent marijuana haze. He was chubbier than he appeared in his photograph that featured on *Turbo*'s website.

The lights had been dimmed in the tiny apartment, and there was a half-empty bottle of Puerto Rican rum next to the beanbag he was sprawled out on. I had to speak over the music – Mohsen Namjoo's elegiac 'Zolf' – to make myself heard. And when I did, the usual happened: a fucking trifecta of incomprehension, disbelief and panic.

It took a hundred implorations and reassurances of the lack of devious intent – or, for that matter, the wherewithal to accomplish it – to tamp down his anxiety. Rishabhh lit a slender low-tar cigarette with trembling hands, as he listened tentatively to who I was and why I was at his place on that cool, breezy evening.

'Fuck! It's . . . my god. Yes, yes, we should pursue the motorcycle. You know I meant to write back to you . . . but there was just too much work.'

'Thank you! I–'

'I need some water . . . I'll just–' said Rishabhh and bolted out of the room, fleeing his own home. I caught up with him just as he burst into a cafe down the road from his apartment complex. Rishabhh's attire – a pair of boxers and a half-sleeved T-shirt, and no footwear – piqued the curiosity of the cafe's patrons, and a flock of titters flew out towards him. He stood near the door for a brief moment and then bolted once again and didn't stop until he was back in the apartment complex. Once there, he made his way into the complex's well-tended, sprawling lawn and slumped on to the ground.

I looked around and upon seeing the coast was clear, I tried to reason with him.

'Go away!' he said. He was out of breath and sweating mildly.

'I know all of this sounds bloody unbelievable, but here I am. Look, it's fine if you think I don't exist, but the bike does. Believe me! And we will have a blast riding it.'

'Fuck.'

'Listen, I'm going to go back to your place and wait for you there. And once again, I mean you no harm – I'm just a motorcycle lover like you are.'

'Okay, yeah, yeah, please go. I'll come later.'

I wasn't expecting Rishabhh to be back so soon, but there he was, early the next morning, and he was calling out for me.

'I'm right here, on the sofa.'

'I'm sorry about last night. I mean this is completely tangential, but have you ever seen turquoise slugs?'

'No, I don't think so. I mean, there are lots of them in Kollengode, black ones, brown ones, speckled ones . . .'

'Ah . . . okay. But you know, I'm just going to crash for a bit, yeah? And that bike, I can't get it out of my head. I've always been fond of Velocettes. We will do something. Hopefully, you'll be around when I wake up?'

I told Rishabhh that he might have been smoking some good shit, but I was really here and was not going anywhere. Rishabhh laughed nervously, and a little later I heard him collapse on to his bed.

So, it looked like I was finally on. Of course, things could still go wrong, but I thought I'd tackle that shit when it happened. The bit about the turquoise slugs was rather weird, but nothing compared to what I had subjected him to.

Since sleep proved elusive, I picked up a copy of *My Uncle Oswald* from the bookshelf and enjoyed Roald Dahl's company until Rishabhh woke up and stumbled into the hall. His bleary eyes panned across the room. It appeared as if he was trying to reconcile the mundanity of that cool morning with blurry, fantastical memories of the previous night that still lapped his consciousness. Then, he saw the book floating in the air.

'Is that Roald Dahl?' he said, once he had recovered his composure.

I laughed. 'Did you know Dahl was a biker boy? He has written some wonderful stuff about his first motorcycle – an Ariel 500cc.'

'Oh really? I've read some of his other stuff; he talks about Oswald's Bentley, I think. You find some brilliant cars in these books and comics. I love all those planes and cars in Tintin!'

'Yeah, I freak out on King Ottokar's Packard Super Eight coupe. Hergé had an exquisite eye for detail!'

'Absolutely. Let me get some coffee.'

It was mildly sunny outside, and light – the colour of lager – illuminated the apartment's living room. It always felt good to be among people who got you, I thought, and walked into the kitchen where Rishabhh was working a French press.

'Goodness, the aroma . . .' I said.

'You've never had coffee, right?'

'No.'

'That's fucking sad, dude. No coffee, no beef fry, no whisky, no sex . . . Fuck, what a life.'

'Yes, but at least I have motorcycles.'

'True, true. Motorcycles. But, dude, you are basically powerless, yeah? You can't hit, or, I don't know, incinerate someone you don't like, right?'

'No. All I can do is read and ride. There are days when I feel like mowing down everyone around me, but I'm powerless to translate any evil thoughts into action, or, to be more specific, cause physical harm to anyone. Whoever imagined me up decided that I'd just be this virtuous, one-dimensional fuck smiling beatifically at the world around him, and that's how it has always been.'

'You know, I've always been open to the possibility that we – and by that I mean humans – could be worshipping highly sentient beings from other galaxies who visited earth thousands of years ago. For all you know, they are still among us. You could be one of them. This is, of course, not one of my original thoughts. You're familiar with von Däniken?'

'*Chariot of the Gods*?'

'Yes, I'm a big fan. What do you think?' said Rishabhh, as we made our way back into the drawing room.

Erich von Däniken had made for engaging reading, I said, but I had no memories of another home. Kollengode, despite its busybodies, was it for me as far back as it went. But I also wondered whether the very concept of memory, as humans understood it, applied to me. Until fairly recently, I was what I had always been – unchanging, and unenriched by any kind of association with anyone; a forlorn monolith erected by man. If you are what you have always been, what do you look back on? It felt like I was perennially preserved in the amber of human imagination.

'It's kind of funny. I remember everything, but until recently, there was nothing worth recollecting.'

'Good you've got bikes.'

'Yes, being obsessed with bikes has changed everything for me. To be consumed by something, I think, is the best gift anyone could ask for. It can make life – even an eternal one – seem shorter than it actually is.'

Rishabhh pursed his lips and nodded. He then sat upright on the sofa.

'Dude, I was thinking about this yesterday, and I'm sorry to break it to you, but I never saw the Thruxton HT,' he said, staring straight into his mug of coffee.

I thought he was kidding.

'You wrote about it in the article . . .' I said.

'I made the whole thing up: that fat man and those nine moles and that bike – they all came out of here,' he said, pointing to his head. 'Don't ask me how it happened. All I know is I was spectacularly stoned and wanted to get done with the article.'

'I'm sorry, but I didn't quite get you . . .'

'See, dude, I think I know how to hook a reader with the very first sentence of my articles, but the endings are always fucking tough.' The mysterious guy and a mysterious bike, Rishabhh said, made for a poignant ending. It left, he said, making an air quote with his fingers, 'the reader hanging', as if that was supposed to be a good thing.

I sat back on the sofa and made Rishabhh repeat himself several times and then crumpled to the ground and began crying.

The last time I cried so much was when Koman died. Later that night after he was cremated and after

I'd dropped an inconsolable Gopi home, I stumbled through Kollengode, crying silently. It was also the night I tried to end my life a second time.

I snuck into Koman's home and rolled our Bullet out of the courtyard, and once I was at a safe distance from his home, I rode like mad towards the railway track, preparing to violently intersect the path of a long-distance train that would dismissively blast past Kollengode station three times a week. I did accomplish what I had set out to do, but as the train clenched itself to a halt and sparks flew all around, I realized that while motorcycles might help me endure life, they could not help me end it.

It was a while before I hauled myself out of that benumbing trough at Rishabhh's that day. I heard the twittering of birds – it felt like a drizzle of honey; an aged mother and her daughter quarrelling in a neighbouring apartment; and a motorcycle, in all probability, a single cylinder with an exhaust baffle, blast down the road opposite Rishabhh's apartment complex.

'Dude, are you okay? Listen, I'm sorry but I didn't want to string you along, so–'

I sniffled and requested Rishabhh to hit Google for details on the earliest flight to Coimbatore. I would reach Kollengode by sundown and let my home wrap itself like a shroud around me. But before that, I wanted to know something.

'Don't you think it is a sign, Rishabhh? You make up this man and this motorcycle you have never heard of, and now it turns out they could actually exist.'

Rishabhh screwed up his face and violently shook his head.

'No, no, no . . . random shit. Just a coincidence.'

I persisted resolutely for the next half an hour, even when Rishabhh marched inside the bathroom to relieve himself and freshen up. He and I were possibly the only two bikers who were privy to motorcycling's greatest secret, I said. We would have fun, riding across India on some nice new bike – the Enfield Interceptor, maybe! – and I would help him think of a way to turn the whole saga into a story he could sell to his editor. I was whiny and I was desperate.

'It will be a crazy ride, Rishabhh. Right across the country: woffoooooooorrrrr!'

'Shut up!' said Rishabhh, as he exited the bathroom and banged the door shut. He wiped his feet on the doormat, marched inside the bedroom and proceeded to change.

'Look, I know this is a very unusual request, but if I were you I would jump at the chance to blast across the hinterland in search of a classic that's lost to history.'

'Stop! I am not jumping because I am not you. And I don't care about these fucking bikes and cars. Ducatis, Yamahas, Zondas, Triumphs, Ferraris, Lamborghini . . . I care a rat's arse for all of this shit!'

Rishabhh's vehemence almost toppled me over, and my shocked silence begged for further elaboration.

'You obviously think I'm a major car lover, right?' Rishabhh said, as he walked back into the drawing room and lit a joint.

'I'm sorry, but I can just about tolerate these things. I feel nauseous if I drive fast. I think it's some kind of strange motion sickness. My GERD only aggravates it.

'And parking, I can never get it right,' he said, shaking his head and smiling, seemingly amused at his own ineptitude.

Why the fuck was he working with an automobile magazine if he didn't like cars or bikes? He was still trying to figure out his life, Rishabhh told me. And it was a good life. He travelled business class to new car launches across the world every other month, stayed at fancy hotels, he 'really' only worked a week a month and got paid 'okay' money.

'And the gifts! I just got the latest Apple iWatch from Hyundai. Imagine that,' he said. 'And the air miles. I am at Lufthansa Senator at the moment, but by next year I should have the Honorary Circle card.'

I told Rishabhh I didn't believe him. His articles made it seem he was always high on exhaust fumes.

'Bro, it's all about manufacturing enthusiasm for cars and bikes. I can do cynical enthusiasm, mellow enthusiasm, rabid enthusiasm, enthusiasm for automotive nostalgia, you know, like, bluff my way around cars and bikes. Actually, I can bluff about anything. I am a man who stands for nothing, but it's okay as long as I'm having fun.'

Despite being among you guys for aeons, I don't think I have any special insights into this grand theatre of life. If you want to know why some people do the things they do, or don't do, I am not the person to ask. Besides, as you are aware, I have my own shit to figure. I think I was justified in doing what I did that morning, though. It was uncharacteristic of me, but I launched into the bastard because I couldn't bear the thought that a whole new generation of automotive lovers was being shaped by this duplicitous twat who didn't possibly know – or care – who John Surtees was, and couldn't tell a disc brake rotor from a clutch plate. The bastard was betraying the spirit of motorcycling, and I told him that I wouldn't let him fuck around with motorcycles.

I hurled the Roald Dahl I was reading a little while earlier at him. The book caught him smack in the face.

'Dude! Chill. Fucker, you just said you were not the violent type!' Rishabhh cried, as he darted into the bathroom and shut the door.

I yelled at him to come out and face me, and when he stayed put inside the bathroom, I hurled more tomes at the glass-frosted bathroom door: a Julian Barnes, a Roberto Calasso, a James Lee Burke, a Paulo Coelho . . .

'Stop it! Fucking lunatic . . .' Rishabhh emerged from the bathroom. He was crying.

'What is happening to me! I'm paying for my sins. I'm sorry, Alisha and Cinderella.'

I placed Ryszard Kapuscinski's *Travels with Herodotus* back on the shelf. What indeed was wrong with him? I didn't want to say anything trite – whatever it was, it sounded like a mess – so I let Rishabhh bawl for a bit, and then, in one of those moments when he stopped bleating, I told him that if he wanted to talk about it, I would be right there, willing to lend a non-judgemental, empathetic ear.

It took him some time to speak coherently, but once he started talking, I wanted to have a go at one of his joints.

Here's why he was sorry:

Alisha Motwani, a freelance illustrator, was not just another notch on Rishabhh Mehtaa's bedpost;

he knew she was different the first time they met. They had been seeing each other for three years and had even discussed marriage. But then came along Cinderella Sequeira. Rishabhh had met Cindy, a corporate communications professional, in Delhi, at the launch of some car or the other, and had hit it off with her. A month later she was in Varanasi, where Rishabhh had booked a room at the Taj.

'So you slept with her?'

'Not really, I mean, I . . . we didn't really do it because–'

My head reels even as I say this, but Rishabhh just couldn't get it up that night because he had his doubts about Cinderella's breasts. He was not sure if they were real or fake. It was a doubt that wriggled inside his head the entire night, and the next morning before she woke up, he was already out on the road, driving in a daze towards Chunar.

It had been over a month since that day – October 1 – but he had broken off all contact with Cinderella, and now there he was, wracked by guilt for having cheated on his sweetheart, and for having abandoned another lady without having offered any explanation. Plus, there was also the humiliation, self-inflicted, of course, of not having been able to get going that night.

Now, I had to ask the obvious question.

How could he be so sure?

'Dude, I know breasts, okay? I curate mammaries here,' he said, tapping his finger on his head. 'I have, like, a PhD on the subject. Hers were too good to be true. Without any blemishes. After I came back from Varanasi, I researched it deeply. I spoke to plastic surgeons; I read up. Do you know what fake breasts are like to the touch?'

'No.'

'Cold. Clammy. And they don't jiggle. Do you get what I mean?'

'If you say so.'

The ending to the article on Varanasi was his way of protesting against all the deceit in the world, including his own, he said.

'I was a wreck that day, completely conflicted. I still don't know why I wrote what I wrote, but maybe, at a deeper level, I was getting back at this world in which nobody is who they appear to be, including myself. A fake world, I thought that day, deserved an article with a fake ending.'

'Don't tell me you were aware of Velocette's failed attempt to build a four-cylinder engine?' I said, referring to a project started by Bertie Goodman's father Percy back in the 1950s. 'Is that how you came up with the idea of featuring a four-cylinder Velo in your article?'

'I was. I proofread all sorts of articles here, and a year or two ago, someone had written a story on it. But don't ask me how I imagined up Chowfin Singh. I have no idea, and now I'm scared.'

This is where this story should have ended. I had no business coercing a man, who was evidently, as they say in Kollengode, a little loose in the head to accompany me in my, for all practical purposes, decidedly outrageous quest. I should have gone home, but, instead, I did something I'm not especially proud of. I told Rishabhh that while I commiserated with him on the unfortunate turn his life had taken, there was no going back for me. He had to come along with me.

'If you don't,' I said, 'I'll write to Alisha and tell her exactly what happened a month ago in Varanasi. I'll also supply her the date on which you were booked at the Taj along with Cinderella.'

I never thought I'd stoop so low, but that's the thing, we are all not as nice as we think we are.

'Are you blackmailing me?'

'You could say that. I really don't want to do this, but there is no other way.'

'Fuck you! You don't even exist, and you think you can have your way with me!'

I told Rishabhh that he had an hour to make up his mind, and disregarding his fulminations, I got back to reading Roald Dahl. Rishabhh stormed out of his apartment, but he was back within the hour.

'Are you fucking there?'

'Yes.'

'I'll do it. What do I have to do?'

'Just do as I say.'

11

I have been to some wonderful places across the world. Rajgir, in Bihar, is not one of them. But I will remember Rajgir as long as I'm around, because it was in that shithole that I was shown the way forward. Wait, I'm getting ahead of myself, so let me tell you how Rishabhh and I found ourselves there in the first place.

Things came together so rapidly after I'd pulled off that sneaky stunt that morning at Rishabhh's place that I really thought there was a god.

The next day, under my supervision, Rishabhh, switching into enthusiast mode, breathlessly filled in his editor, who had been away on a holiday, on the legend of the Velocette that he had sighted in Varanasi and sold him a grand plan that could also pull in some money for the magazine.

He said the mail sent by KK Swamy, 'that extremely knowledgeable chap in Kerala', and his subsequent chats with him – as well as judicious research – had convinced him that he was on the trail of a global scoop. His 'Blast from the Fast' series would regularly update the magazine's readers – via its website, Instagram and Facebook – on his pursuit of a motorcycle that no one had written about before. He would start in Allahabad, where its rider hailed from, or perhaps Amritsar, from where they would barrel down the Grand Trunk Road and document, along the way, India's fading but still significant British motorcycling heritage. He said he had already activated the magazine's classic bike network across the country, just in case the rider was spotted in a different part of India, and, if that happened, he would air-dash to the nearest city, get a bike arranged from a friendly motorcycle manufacturer and resume the hunt.

It didn't take too long for his avuncular editor and publisher, a Parsi named Rohinton Cooper, to green-light the plan. The moneyed Cooper, who was aware of Velocette's four-cylinder project, was a genuine enthusiast, the sort of man whose heart sank at the sight of abandoned automobiles. He called up a few highly placed friends of his at lubricant companies, and a sponsorship deal was quickly signed with the magazine. Twenty days later, we were tunnelling through the early morning fog on the Grand Trunk Road from Amritsar on a silver-grey Royal Enfield Himalayan, which was outfitted with panniers, luggage racks and a windscreen, and plastered with Castrol decals.

My last really big, uninterrupted ride had been with Koman back in the 1960s, and, as a motorcyclist, I was eager to reacquaint myself with the many nuances of light; to see the world from tens of different angles; and to submit to the magnetic pull of the horizon. Rishabhh, who took his time trusting my skills as a rider, kept to himself when we started out, but his surliness dissipated when I offered to take over writing duties for the website and the magazine.

And so, we hauled in the miles, capturing in photographs, videos, and suitably breathless prose, some very memorable machines on either side of the ancient highway: an Ariel W/NG 350 in Jalandhar, a BSA A65 Star in Ambala, a Goldstar in Delhi, a Norton Commando in Kanpur. In Allahabad, a city I had last visited some forty years ago to reconfirm Kadar's story, we dined with a retired bureaucrat named U.K. Mishra, who had this gorgeous 1960 Norton Dominator Model 99, and whose left shoulder twitched every couple of minutes with Tourettic regularity.

Rishabhh spoke like a pro with Mishra, tiptoeing cleverly around the periphery of the vast subject of British motorcycles, inventing the story of an uncle who rode a Norton Atlas, and prodding the old man's fading memory. On my behalf, he also asked Mishra, who had once owned a string of Nortons, including Dominators, about whether early Dommies were indeed afflicted with lubrication problems. The Dominators of the late 1940s, Mishra said, ran a dry clutch, but since all of Norton's bikes were chain-run, you had to lube them every 800 or so kilometres. Mishra said that the real improvement came in the mid-1950s with the Norton Atlas, but he was also of the view – and I was in silent consonance with him on this – that it was BSA which revolutionized the 1960s' engine scene with its parallel twins.

Both Mishra and Angad Chauhan, the city's go-to classic motorcycle mechanic who joined us for dinner that night, recalled the spare parts store owned by Gurjit Singh, and still spoke, in hushed tones, about the calamity that had wiped out his family, but they couldn't really add anything further to what we already knew about him. The site of the Singh & San's spare parts store, they told us, was now occupied by a large supermarket.

Three days after our meeting with Mishra, we were in Rajgir, after winging by Varanasi and Bodhgaya. Rajgir was not part of our original plan, but Rishabhh forced me to take a detour because he had sold an article on the Buddhist Circuit to a travel magazine and wanted to check out 'the ancient capital of Magadha' before we hit the Grand Trunk Road again.

For the first time since we left Amritsar, I had to confront the fact that none of the classic bike owners or famed mechanics we had met along the way had encountered the rider and the motorcycle we were searching for. I spent a whole afternoon wondering if I would ever find myself in Chowfin Singh's slipstream, and then reluctantly accompanied Rishabhh on his evening stroll around Rajgir. A melancholy twilight had started to seep into the dreary town. I was tetchy and wanted to get done with Rajgir as soon as possible, and felt relieved when Rishabhh decided to head back to our lodge, after desultorily surveying the crumbling ruins and stupas around the town and poking his head into mud huts and sweetmeat shops that swarmed with fat flies.

That was when a decrepit old man materialized next to Rishabhh.

'Namaste, babuji, do you want guide? My name is Bun Babu.'

Bun Babu wore a tattered kurta and his thick spectacle lenses magnified cloudy eyes. He walked with such a pronounced stoop that he resembled a sickle.

'No thanks, we are done,' Rishabhh said curtly.

'Babuji, the way I know Rajgir, no one does; from the Buddha to Bimbisara to Ajatshatru, and–'

'Boss, we don't need a guide. We are heading back to our hotel,' Rishabhh said, quickening his pace.

'No problem, babuji, but can I ask you something?'

'What?'

'Are you searching for something?'

'No. Why don't you get lost?'

I stopped walking and turned around. The old man was still hobbling behind us.

'I think you should speak to–' I told Rishabhh.

'What? You seriously think that this has something to do with that bike–'

'I don't know, but talk to him. At the very least, you'll get a good quote for your story.'

Rishabhh swallowed his exasperation and waited for the guide to catch up, and when he did, he told him rather dramatically, 'Who among us is not searching for something, Bun Babuji? Everyone is.'

'No, babuji, I am talking about something specific.'

'Like what?'

The guide craned his neck and fixed Rishabhh with an unblinking stare. The cataracts in his eyes cleared up, and he stood erect with his chest out. When he spoke again, he was a different man with a different voice.

In crisp British-accented English, and in a stentorian tone, he said, 'I don't know what you are looking for, laddie, but whatever it is, you won't find it here. Go further east, towards the great mountain with five peaks. But remember, ultimately your search begins where everybody else's ends. Cheers.'

And then he dropped down dead. A horrified Rishabhh, along with a few curious onlookers, tried to revive the guide, but the geriatric was gone. Someone from the crowd called up someone from his family, and within ten minutes several members of his brood came running. Rishabhh and I left as the wailing started.

We didn't speak a word to each other on our way back to the lodge.

'What have you landed me into, you dickhead!' he said once we were back in the room.

For the briefest of moments, I wondered – yet again – about the ethics of dragging Rishabhh along for a journey that looked like it would be an extraordinary one. Bun Babu, I was certain, was a signpost! But what if something happened to Rishabhh? I might be a bastard at times, but I didn't want anything to happen to the poor guy.

I looked at Rishabhh. He was glued to his phone, chatting with Alisha. I saw him smile into the phone.

Breast-obsessed scumbag, I thought, and, more importantly, fake enthusiast! And a loony. I mean, if I were in his place, I'd have got my head checked at a shrink's instead of allowing myself to be bossed around by a disembodied voice. Then again, it was a good thing he was a little touched in the head. Later, when we learnt to tolerate each other better, I would discover that he was certain the appearance of turquoise slugs on earth was the first sign of an impending apocalypse. One of his former girlfriends, a Wiccan, had convinced him about it. His apparently recently acquired pudginess, he said, was the handiwork of a pair of fat twins he teased and bullied at school. 'Mehul and Vipul Shah. I think I started gaining weight the day I met those obese fucks at a reunion. They stay close to my place and each time I run into them, they look at me and exchange these sly glances. It's them, I know it, those chuts are doing something to me,' Rishabhh told me, lifting up his T-shirt and grabbing a fold of his belly fat. Well, I thought, he deserved to be with me on that journey.

'Rishabhh, the "great mountain with five peaks" is the Kanchenjunga . . .' I said.

'Yes! But stop doing this sound projection thing. Why can't you just talk to me? It freaks me out!'

'Okay, sorry, but we are going to Gangtok,' I said.

I thought Rishabhh would put up a stout resistance to the sudden change in plan, but the fucker simply loved Alisha way too much, I guess.

I asked for the laptop, quickly wrote a bunch of bloaty articles on the mechanicals of some of the British motorcycles we had encountered and asked him to send the same along with a bunch of photos and short vids to the guys at *Turbo* so they could keep the website updated. Rishabhh informed his excited editor that the motorcycle had been sighted in Gangtok, and that he was dashing there right away.

And then, the next morning, we rocketed down National Highway 1 to Calcutta, and reached there just in time to catch the overnight Darjeeling Mail to Jalpaiguri. From Jalpaiguri, we rode up the mountains past Kurseong and Darjeeling, and entered Gangtok on an evening of idle rain and empty streets.

With its unvarnished walls and empty sockets, Hotel Karma was not much of a hotel, but Rishabhh was desperate for some warmth and so we rode straight in.

'Welcome, sir, welcome, I was waiting for you,' said its owner, a lanky man who wore a beautiful fedora.

'I'm sorry, but how did you know . . .'

'No, no, sir, this is how I like to greet my guests. This is a new hotel, and you are among the first people to come here,' said the owner. He seemed to be the only one around.

Rishabhh chose a room on the second floor and was about to ascend the stairs when the lights went out.

'Oh no, electricity is always causing problems. Problems, problems . . .' said the owner, as he groped inside one of the shelves for a candle.

'Sir, please use the torch on your mobile and be on your way. I'll get the generator going. Room no. 222.'

I decided to check on the Himalayan before we called it a day and ventured outside, but a blood-curdling scream brought me right back inside the hotel.

It was Rishabhh, and his voice seemed to grow fainter with each passing second. I glanced at the owner. He was eating his dinner by the light of a candle. He looked up conspiratorially and continued eating. I rushed up the stairs and into room no. 222, and realized that I was plunging into an abyss.

12

I don't know what day it is, Ooshie, but it's such a lovely day. It's quiet and cool and nice. I got up early, read the newspaper and had breakfast. I also had my two pegs of rum and Coca-Cola at noon. The maid has just left. I have to have lunch now, but I don't feel like having it. I don't know if I am feeling tired, but I'm lying in bed. I'm not tired, I just want to lie down.

Today, I sat gazing at the sea and thought about the first time we met, and foolishly felt our lives would start all over again. You remember that evening, Ursula? Kit Kat, 14 January 1970. That was when I first saw you. You were seated at the far end of the restaurant with Rosemary. It was the band's first day at Kit Kat. They wanted us to play stuff like at Berry's and Venice at the Astoria.

You were wearing a pale blue dress and your hair was

tied up in a bun, and you kept looking at Eustace. I was nervous, trying hard to concentrate on the piano, and I kept wondering, 'Men, why is she looking at him?'

We played well that day, no? What did we play? Something from South Pacific*?* My Fair Lady*? I don't remember anything except for 'Lullaby of Birdland'. That was when you first looked at me. Eustace, Mark Antony and me, all macapaos from Bandra, we put up a good show. After the tea session got over, Eustace introduced you to me. 'Meet Ursula, she's my cousin sister,' he said. I smiled at you and felt happy. Then we walked you and Rosemary to Marine Lines and hurried back in a cab to prepare for the dinner session.*

~

Rishabhh and I have no idea what happened inside room no. 222 at Hotel Karma. All we remember is screaming at the top of our voices, and at the other end of our screams, as it were, was a small restaurant.

Three musicians – a pianist, a bass guitarist and a drummer – stood frozen on a raised platform to the right of a blue door. They were dressed in white shirts, black trousers and lemon-coloured ties. There were many patrons clumped around the tables, but they were an amorphous mass, always at the edge of my vision, just like the liveried waiters who swum through the narrow channels of space inside the cramped restaurant. For some reason, I could never see anyone clearly, except for two young, beautiful ladies who were seated at a far corner of the restaurant. One of them waved to the bass guitarist, animating the tableau for the briefest of instants. Every couple of seconds the entire restaurant would vanish before reappearing, and with every reappearance, it would change almost imperceptibly. The colour of the walls changed from blue to grey and then back to the original colour, and a small marble water fountain appeared intermittently in front of the stage. We heard the melodious trickle of music from the piano, and then everything became quiet as before. The musicians walked towards the two young girls. The pianist smiled shyly at one of them, and the group walked out of the door. Rishabhh and I followed them out.

~

Eustace is no more, by the way. Nothing dramatic, he went to sleep at night and never woke up. That is how I, too, want to die. A week before he died, Eustace and I attended a mass for musicians on the Feast Day of St Cecilia. After communion we prayed for the souls of Benny

Rozario, Johnny Rodricks, Maurice Concessio, Cosmos Fernandes, Trini and many others. Next year Eustace will also be added to that illustrious list. Perhaps, I, too, will be on it. You know how Eustace was, no? Right after mass ended, the bugger suggested we go to town. I was tired but I went anyway. It was Eustace, after all. So we took a cab and went to Marine Lines, to Chez Nous. Remember Chez Nous? It's still the same, Ooshie. It's dark and cosy; it still has those curvy tables. The manager told me that apart from the cloth covering on the walls, nothing has changed. But they don't serve chicken spaghetti and filet mignon any more. We sat there for a long time, two old men at an old haunt, talking about old times.

I really like Chez Nous. We used to go there nearly once every month, and the kids, they also liked it, no? We finished very late at Chez Nous that day, but you know how Eustace is – he told the cab driver to drive us around town before getting back to Bandra. So, that's what we did. We passed Churchgate, Flora Fountain, Kala Ghoda, Regal – Ooshie, do you remember the first movie we watched together? It was at Liberty Theatre. I can't remember the name of the movie, or the actors. There's just this one scene from the movie that keeps playing in my head. We bought tickets for it in black, remember?

~

Outside the restaurant, the light was failing, but as soon as we stepped out, Rishabhh and I had the sense of being in a city that was intensely familiar and yet coldly hostile.

'Is this Bombay? Dhobi Talao? Dude, I can't make out anything.'

It did appear, inexplicably, that we were back in Bombay, or, perhaps, I thought, in a likeness of it. Everything around us seemed once removed, and it felt like we were inhabiting a faint reflection of Bombay. Like the patrons of the restaurant, the city around us lacked definition, and its venerable edifices hung over us like impending rain.

We followed the four youngsters past a theatre that looked like Metro. But why couldn't we read the marquee signs? Why was the theatre empty? Why were the pianist and his friends the only people on the sidewalk? We passed an Irani restaurant, where I saw a gentleman at one of the tables surreptitiously remove two paos from his pocket and sit down to eat his fried eggs. The statue of some Parsi grandee gazed resolutely ahead at the huge gates of a hotel across the street, and then we spotted the boundary wall of a suburban railway station.

'That's Marine Lines! Marine Lines, bro. Can we catch a train and go home?'

Even as we both quickened our pace, I was struck by a disturbing sensation that we had perhaps trespassed on someone else's city, a deeply personal Bombay. The thoroughfares and streets around us ended abruptly, swallowed by darkness; I saw more buildings that gave me a sense of Bombay, but they all seemed to be hollow, uninhabited shells. Every street around us was empty except for the one on which the musicians and their two lady friends were walking. The Bombay we were in appeared to be built solely for the pianist and the lady he was besotted with. I wanted to convey my apprehension to Rishabhh but before I could do that, we were transported to a graveyard, where an indistinct group of mourners stood around a freshly dug grave. Like the people in the restaurant, these men and women, too, were faceless, except for a brooding old man who stood with his hands folded. Over the next couple of minutes, as Rishabhh showered me with the choicest abuses, several vivid worlds quietly built themselves around us and then vanished. A grand church sprang up from nowhere, and we found ourselves inside it, sitting next to the old man for Mass; the next instant we were in a cab with him and another man, who, I suppose, was his friend, and all of us hurtled across the Mahim Causeway. Then, as if someone had flipped a page of the man's life, we sat next to him as he drank to his friend's health in a dimly lit restaurant, and then boom! Everything went impenetrably dark and sepulchrally quiet.

A low hubbub rose around us, big city noises set against the velvety darkness. And then a voice rose above the noise. It was a man's voice, and it sought only those ears that were meant to hear it.

'*Do ka dus. Do ka dus*,' he said. He seemed within earshot, and yet appeared to be always moving.

Hindi, like for most people from Kerala, is not my strongest suit, and I stood there like an alpaca for a bit, until Rishabhh explained to me that the guy appeared to be a black marketeer in cinema tickets, and that, in typical Bombay style, he was furtively offering patrons tickets that cost two rupees ('do') for ten rupees ('dus').

But why were the tickets so cheap? Even Thangaraj, that dilapidated, bedbug-infested dump in Kollengode, charges, I think, around eighty bucks! So . . .

'Does that mean we've . . .'

'Gone back in time? Oh fucking god!' Rishabhh said.

We heard the man's voice again. This time, though, it appeared as if he was joined by more of his kind, a leash of black marketeers.

'*Do ka dus, do ka dus . . .*' Their sales pitch encircled us, growing louder steadily, and then splintering into disjointed echoes. It all seemed to be a wicked parody of one of Hindi cinema's numerous melodramatic scenes in which a guilt-ridden/distraught/lovelorn hero or heroine is assaulted by a hundred different voices, and we had to eventually stick our fingers in our ears to shut the voices out.

'Buy the damn ticket!' I yelled over the din.

'I lost everything!! My wallet, my phone!'

'Give him something! I can't bear this any more.'

Rishabhh timed his expression of interest in the black marketeers' wares to coincide with the briefest of lulls between their relentlessly loud pitches.

'Arre boss,' said Rishabhh, 'give me a ticket. I don't have money, but I have a nice watch.'

The maelstrom of noise subsided. I heard the shuffle of feet.

'Watch? Is it Titoni?'

'No, no. Seiko.'

'Japan? Not Swiss. Okay, it'll do. Give me the watch, take your ticket.'

'Okay, but which movie is playing here?'

'Arre, come on, you are joking, right? You are buying a ticket, and you don't know the name of the picture?'

'No, I don't. Really.'

'You are a strange man, partner. But don't worry, you'll enjoy watching the picture. Trust me, you will never see anything like it again. I'll be on my way now, too many cops around here.'

'Bhaisahab, where's the theatre?'

'Are you blind? You are standing right in front of it.'

'What?'

We heard the man walk away, softly chuckling to himself. As his footsteps faded, the darkness around us slowly turned to light, and there we were, standing right in front of Liberty Theatre.

It was early evening, rush hour in Bombay, and perhaps time for the evening show. But there was no one around us. The Bombay we were in was uncharacteristically still and insufferably quiet.

'Now?' Rishabhh said.

'Let's go and watch the movie. What else is there to do?' I said.

'Screw you! You and your bloody plan . . .' he said, but entered the art deco theatre all the same.

We walked past empty booking counters and a forlorn soda fountain. The recessed lighting on the ceiling of the lobby and the bands of lighting along its edges flickered as we ascended the carpeted staircase and entered the cool, dark, empty auditorium. A jaundiced, anaemic beam of light directed Rishabhh towards the centre of the auditorium, and we both took our seats.

'Did they play the national anthem back then?' Rishabhh asked me.

'No, back then we were a more civilized country.'

'That's good. I hate getting up after I've sat down,' he said and laughed a little too exuberantly at his own joke.

There were a few annoyed murmurs from the back rows. Rishabhh and I turned around to investigate the source of the noise, but we could see no one. It was all very strange, but at least it was in keeping with the general scheme of things, I thought, as the golden curtain rose and the screen flickered to life.

Surprisingly, there were no opening credits, or even the mandatory unfurling of the film's name accompanied by the clash of cymbals – the audience was thrown right into what appeared to be an important scene.

Four men, three of whom wore double-breasted suits, sat on four different couches in a massive hall with green walls and just too many pillars, their barely concealed distaste of each other congealing on the heavily carpeted floor.

Six ornate chandeliers spilled a garish brightness

all over, and a spiral staircase, which appeared to have sprouted out of the centre of the room, went nowhere. In the distance, behind a sheer curtain, four ladies shimmied to a kind of low, rumbling tribal beat, and about eight men, wearing Turkish fezes and carrying rifles, guarded the hall.

It looked like a gangster's den, early 1970s' Bollywood, but both Rishabhh and I were unfamiliar with the actors. One of the suits got up and walked to the bar. He poured himself a peg of Vat 69 whisky and gulped it down.

'Dilawar said seven. It's already seven-thirty! How much longer do we have to wait?' he said, glowering at his empty whisky glass.

'Kartar, Kartar, my brother . . .' a voice boomed out from the entrance of the hall. A tall, swarthy man, obviously the tardy Dilawar, wearing an off-white three-piece suit and oversized sunglasses, strode into the room. He was flanked by two well-built men dressed in sheer shirts and bell-bottom trousers.

'Kartar, my friend . . .' Dilawar said, smiling at his tetchy guest, and clasping him by the elbow. 'Never willing to wait. Always impatient. To get going, to rule Bombay – patience is a virtue, Kartar, especially in this line of business.'

'Gentlemen,' he said, addressing the others,

'I apologize for being late, but you know how unpredictable this city is. Let's quickly get down to why I've called you here. Come on, let us . . .'

Dilawar led the four suits down the corridor into a boardroom sort of place.

'Mike, Raka,' he said before shutting the door of the boardroom, 'I don't want anyone to disturb us, okay?'

His bull-like bodyguards nodded.

Dilawar sat at the head of a long table inside the boardroom and lit a cigarette.

'He had called,' he said.

'Oh my god!' said Kartar. He reached into his jacket pocket and took out a pack of cigarettes.

'What did He say?' one of the other men asked. He was a distinguished-looking elderly man. He wore a cravat and had long, bony fingers.

'Ebenezer sahab, He wanted to know if we could help Him with something. I said of course!'

'Of course! This is an absolute honour, a privilege,' said Kartar.

'Yes, if it were not for Him, we wouldn't be sitting here. Inspector Vijay would have got us all. No gold smuggling, no extortion, no nothing. Inspector Vijay!' Ebenezer lit a cigarette and laughed. His laughter had a mocking edge to it, and it rippled across the room, provoking a similar disdainful mirth in its other occupants. They all laughed exaggeratedly, like villains in Hindi movies are wont to do.

'Yes, He showed him his place,' said Dilawar.

'Only He could have done that. Upend the very foundations of a Hindi movie, these pointless films in which everything is either black or white. Good versus evil, wrong versus right. You know what He told me when I approached Him all those years ago? He said His favourite colour was grey.'

'What a man. But tell me one thing, Dilawar, are you sure it was He who got in touch?' The man who asked Dilawar this question had mostly stayed silent till now. He was small and foxlike, and wore a toupee.

'Samuel, once you hear His voice, you know. You don't mistake it for any ordinary voice.'

'What does He want from us?' said Kartar.

'He is looking for someone. A man who is supposedly after a particular motorcycle that He, too, is interested in.'

'A motorcycle? How can that be? What makes Him think that He can find him here? How can anyone get in here?' Kartar said.

'I don't know. You don't ask Him questions. All He said was that if we encountered the man, we were supposed to let Him know.'

'Is that me they are referring to?' Rishabhh said.

'I'd think so. He specifically said "man".'

'But this is a movie, right?'

'I don't know, Rishabhh, I just don't know,' I said, and melted into a puddle of whiny, anxious incomprehension. 'I don't know where we are, I don't know what is happening. I just want to go home and sleep. I'm sorry for getting you involved in all this. All I wanted to do was ride the Thruxton. And now, after all that we've been through, it looks like there's some other guy who's after it.'

I added, 'Perhaps you should have a chat with these guys. I mean, that guy they are talking about seems to be our only hope . . .'

'Talk to them? They are gangsters!'

'It's a movie.'

'Is it?'

'I don't know.'

Someone in the back asked Rishabhh to shut up.

'You shut up, chutiye!'

Then he got up from his seat, took a deep breath, and said, 'Dilawar sahab, I think you are looking for me.'

A few shards of sound – the truncated screech of a harmonium, among others – dropped down into the auditorium, and a collective gasp emanated from the screen. Pistols were drawn and pointed at Rishabhh. Kartar, the most belligerent of the lot, advanced towards him, filling up the screen and issuing vile threats.

'Who are you? How did you get in here? Are you Commissioner Khan's man? Another Inspector Vijay? I swear on my mother, you won't leave this place alive!' he said.

'Blow him apart, Kartar,' said Samuel, jumping out of his chair. 'We don't want to take any chances. Come on, what are you waiting for?'

'Kartar, Samuel, come to your senses! Put your guns away! This can't be Commissioner Khan's man! Inspector Vijay was supposed to be a one-man army. There was nobody else who was a threat to us in the film script. I don't want you to act in haste. We need to ascertain who he is,' said Dilawar, coming between Rishabhh and the barrels of the pistols.

A strained silence descended on the room. Both Samuel and Kartar glared at Dilawar, but ultimately the pistols went back into their jacket pockets and the two capos sat back down like petulant children.

Dilawar turned towards Rishabhh.

'I really hope you are not what my friends think you to be, because if you are, I'll be the first one to kill you,' he said, his eyes boring into Rishabhh.

'No, I'm not Commissioner Khan's man, whoever he is! I'm just . . . I'm just a passer-by!'

'Well, we haven't had anyone in here for a while. But who are you and what are you doing here?'

Rishabhh excised me from his narrative and presented himself as this diehard biker in search of a legendary motorcycle he had spotted in Varanasi. When he finished speaking, Dilawar smiled.

'Interesting, and, gentlemen,' he said, turning towards his fellow gangsters, 'it ties in with what He had told me.' They nodded, some a little more surlily than the others.

'Okay, you wait there,' Dilawar said as he walked towards the other end of the boardroom and dialled a number on the telephone. The conversation he had with the person at the other end of the line was brief, and when he kept the receiver back in its cradle, Dilawar spoke with great urgency.

'Okay, listen carefully. He wants you to head for the sea. Now, if you see it, just jump in. It might not appear again for a long time, that's how it works here. So, go look for Marine Drive, Chowpatty, and He will find you. If you meet Him, let Him know that we, the creatures of imagination and memory, will be forever indebted to Him. Go!' said Dilawar. The dons waved Rishabhh goodbye, and the curtain started falling.

Rishabhh and I darted out of the theatre, only to find ourselves in the middle of a desert. A shrill sunset draped itself over the horizon.

'Dude?' Rishabhh said.

'Let's head west. The sea is towards the west,' I said, and both of us started running. But our exertions were in vain, as the very next moment we found ourselves in what appeared to be the old man's house.

Music seeped out of the computer speakers in his apartment. It was a compelling piano solo, alive and full of joy. The geriatric closed his eyes and listened to the music, as a shoal of poignant moments from, I suppose, his life swam around us.

I saw him come back from an early morning walk. There he was returning home from the airport with his wife. We saw him at his daughter's wedding. With his son in his arms, looking much younger, and with his wife at their wedding. In a dimly lit bar, I saw him as a teenager drinking vodka with his friends. At the Hanging Gardens, in Bombay, with his girlfriend who was gifting him a trouser piece. Holding his parents' hands at a railway station and looking delighted as a passenger train thundered past, and finally as a little boy reluctant to go to school on a rainy day in a place that smelled of wet earth.

By now, I knew that the world we were trapped in

was exactly what I hoped it wouldn't be. But towards the end, though, the reverse chronology became evident. What was playing out around us were the reminiscences of an old man.

Was the bastard's life flashing before him? Did that mean, as is commonly believed, he would die soon? Did that mean the place we were in would also cease to exist? Standing there in the rain in the courtyard of a red-roofed home, I sought an exit out of our host's rapidly ebbing world. If this was as far back as it went for him, it probably meant the end of the journey for us as well.

But then everything kind of dissolved, and slowly in the distance I heard the roar of the sea and saw the familiar promenade of Marine Drive. It was a rainy night, and a man and a woman were walking on the promenade. The man appeared to be asking her something. The woman looked bashful and nodded. They both held hands. Waves crashed against the wall below. I looked beyond the couple at the sea and noticed something moving in the darkness. It was a silver-coloured speedboat. I alerted Rishabhh, and we ran hard into the gusts of wind and leapt headlong right through the couple into the ocean.

~

Mr Oswald Lobo, son of late Primrose and Nelson Lobo, the third child among five children, passed away in Bombay on 30th November, around 1 p.m., aged sixty-five.

Dearest husband of Late Ursula Fernandes (née Lobo).

Dearest father of Adam Lobo (Denver) and Andrea Martin (Dubai).

Dearest brother of late Rudolph, Ronald and Rita.

Funeral services will be held at our Lady of Victories Church in Mahim on 1st December.

May his soul rest in peace, Amen.

13

And so that is how we exited one Bombay for another. But the waters were agitated by a stiff, choppy wind and Marine Drive's glow grew fainter with every passing second.

I scanned the seascape for Rishabhh and saw him flailing in the water. He obviously didn't know how to swim, but before I could begin to worry about his safety, the speedboat appeared out of nowhere and knifed its way towards Rishabhh. By the time I got aboard it, a tall man was administering CPR on Rishabhh, who was lying on a plush bench just behind the wheel of the boat. The man's colleague waited by their side with some towels.

'He will be okay in about five minutes,' the tall man said, and got back behind the wheel.

Rishabhh revived pretty quickly, just as the man

had said. He spat out an enormous amount of water and moaned, but he looked like he would live. His rescuer handed him a set of fresh clothes and some tea from a flask.

'Relax, relax, you're fine. We'll be there soon.'

'Where?' Rishabhh asked feebly.

'Don't worry, relax,' the tall man said, evading the question with a toothy smile.

I asked Rishabhh to take it easy and lie down.

An hour later, the boat docked at a pier. The two men helped Rishabhh on to the jetty and led him towards a car parked on a narrow road. It was an impeccably maintained silver Rolls-Royce, with a hood as long as an insomniac's night. A burly chauffeur emerged from the beautiful car, possibly a 1960s' model, and held the door open for Rishabhh.

'But where am I going? Who are you guys?'

'Please, please . . . don't worry,' said the skipper, as he and his companion firmly but smilingly nudged Rishabhh inside the car.

The driver started the car, and it glided along the dark road.

'I'm with you,' I said.

Rishabhh was startled and spoke a little too loudly, 'But where are we–'

'Need anything, sir?' the chauffeur asked, looking into the rear-view mirror.

'No, no, it's okay. I'm good, everything's fine.'

'Let's talk later,' I told Rishabhh.

He nodded and slumped into the leather seat, and dozed off.

I was both a trifle worried and excited, as I ensconced myself in the plush front passenger seat. My apprehension largely concerned the identity of the man we were going to meet. He looked to be another contender for the world's fastest throne. Would he be an obstacle or another signpost? I also wondered about Kartar and his men. If those were indeed the memories of a dying old man we had unintentionally intruded into, did it mean that the crime lords, too, had ceased to exist?

I slept during most of our journey, and when I woke up I saw that the car had come to a halt in front of a massive gate. The chauffeur got out of the car and spoke through a speakerphone. When the gates opened, we were driven through a road bordered on both sides by casuarina groves on to a clearing about the size of three basketball courts. Three roads radiated from the clearing as if it was almost a roundabout. One of them, narrow and loopy, led up a hillock, the other two meandered in between the casuarina groves.

I got out of the car and saw a huge mansion atop the hillock, and sensed the briny presence of the ocean. We stood there, under the mild morning sun, and intently watched the chauffeur who looked as if he was waiting for a cue to make his exit. An impatient Rishabhh wanted to know where he was, but the chauffeur merely gave him a cold, blank stare. That's when I heard a distinctive rumble and then yet another. The noise, rising up from the two smaller roads that led to the clearing, grew louder and louder until I saw the very creatures capable of producing such gorgeous music. A blood-red Ducati 1198 SP appeared to our left, and on the other side, moving rapidly towards us, ringed by halos of glittering dust, was a black Triumph Daytona 675R. I gazed longingly at the Duc.

A deep, disembodied voice, probably channelled through a hidden speaker on the estate, welcomed Rishabhh inside. The voice wanted Rishabhh to choose one of the two motorcycles and proceed up to the mansion.

I told Rishabhh to pick the Ducati. He reluctantly wore the spare helmet and knee pads offered to him by the Ducati's rider and got astride the motorcycle. I was on the bike in a flash and sized up the Duc which, at idle, sounded like it was gargling gravel. It was big, it was beautiful, and it felt extremely powerful when I twisted my wrist to rev it up. A man stood at the beginning of the road that led up the hillock. He had a green flag and a walkie-talkie. He indicated to Rishabhh to wait just before a thick, white marking line on the road and counted down from three to one, simultaneously waving his green flag. I asked Rishabhh to hold on, shifted into race mode and went full throttle.

Was this a race of some sort? Were we being timed? I had no clue. The only thing that was clear was that the person who was waiting for us up there wanted to gauge the riding ability of his guest, and the better I rode the more inclined he would be towards entertaining Rishabhh. In short, our mysterious host – and the man who presumably played a role in our rescue from the old man's head – was an automobile enthusiast. Like me, like Chowfin Singh, like Koman. Like all those people we had met on our journey from Delhi to Rajgir. And he had a great taste in motorcycles. It would, I thought, be a pleasure getting to know him.

The road that led up the hill was unlike any I had ever seen. It had its fair share of gentle turns, and straights where the Duc sounded like an

Armageddon as I went hard on the gas, all the way to some 252 kph, but every so often the road twisted violently, corkscrewed on itself and then unfurled again, presenting a glorious view of the sea that roared below. Just when I would relax slightly after exiting a perilous bend, the contours of another wicked turn would begin to take shape. Up there on that road, sunlight alternated with shade, the wind bellowed in my ears and gravity waited to grab Rishabhh's ankles and pull rider and bike down into the ocean. I counted at least seven tight corners, but I could have been wrong and there might have been many more. It was a mad road, and after the third corner I told myself, 'Kandakarna, you asked for this; you keep claiming you are a great rider. Now is the time to prove it. Come on, da.'

I went back to the basics. I went in close and shot myself out wide around the corners, applied quick dabs of braking each time I approached one, gathered enough revs as I headed out of a bend, and feathered the rear brakes on inclines. None of this would have been possible, of course, had it not been for Rishabhh who hunched over the motorcycle and shut his eyes. I don't know what he thinks of me, but he had grown to trust in my abilities as a rider and was extremely accommodating on that thrilling scramble up the hill.

I should add here that I was lucky to have been astride the 1198 SP. Its slipper clutch was a revelation. Never had I ridden a large motorcycle that was as stable on downshifts into corners. The Duc read my mind and read it right consistently. In the end, I thought I had done a pretty good job as we headed straight to the porch of the mansion, past a chequered flag waved by a short, slight man who walked up to Rishabhh with a big smile on his face.

'Welcome, sir. Let's go inside,' he told Rishabhh, who was happy to get off the Ducati. I lingered around the Duc for a bit, inhaling a faint mist of tyre smoke, and entered the elegant mansion.

Our mysterious host's taste in motorcycles didn't quite extend to his home. Glitzy chandeliers, faux Victorian furniture, a massive fish tank with garish aquarium fish and an ornate staircase confronted us in the hall. I felt like I was on a Tamil film movie set from the 1970s, and half expected a lachrymose heroine to come running down the stairs any moment.

I also thought that the elaborate tropical garden outside was a needless affectation and were it not for a well-stocked library that led out to a long patio, the bungalow would have been truly unbearable.

But then we were taken to a large, sunlit room that looked as if it had been created to negate the tasteless, ersatz opulence of most of the rest of the mansion. It was sparsely furnished – a wood-panelled bar, two silver-coloured floor-standing speakers and a low-set table that was placed between two muted grey couches. A 2004 Ferrari F1 crankshaft replica sat on the table. I got up from the couch to take a closer look at the coldly beautiful creature.

'Shit! Dude, another chutiya car guy. I'm telling you, bro, he will walk into this room wearing a Ferrari cap, Ferrari driving shoes, Ferrari sunglasses. Like all those juvenile motherfuckers,' Rishabhh muttered, rolling his eyes.

A liveried house help entered the room with a tray that held a cup of coffee and a tiny case. We were both puzzled by the nature of its contents. Why was Rishabhh being offered earplugs? The question was answered a few minutes later – in the form of a prolonged mechanical wail that pierced through the room, its aural slipstream lingering like a bride's train.

I looked at the speakers. Why was our host playing the sound of a Formula One car going at full tilt? That spectacle of sound was followed, after a brief lull, by a clutch of engine notes; of Formula One cars at the start of a race, heaving, impatient, growly; of racing cars accelerating through the gears – long, harsh strips of noise interspersed with snorts and violent pops – and then the three distinct noises started playing out with symphonic precision, each separated from the other by a pinprick of silence.

The speakers' diaphragms throbbed, the windowpanes rattled and the replica of the Formula One car's crankcase shuddered on the table.

Sometimes my intuition is so spot on it surprises me. I firmly dissuaded Rishabhh from picking up the earplugs. It was an attempt to test his love for automobiles, I told him, just as the route up to the mansion was a test to gauge his ability as a rider. Whoever this man was, he was not ordinary, and we stood a better chance of getting out of the mansion if Rishabhh acted like someone who got a hard-on each time he went to the races.

'Fuck,' said Rishabhh, as the sequence of ear-bleeding sounds repeated itself. This time, though, he clenched his teeth and endured it stoically.

We both braced ourselves for the next wave of noise. But what emerged out of the speakers, instead, was Vivaldi's 'Four Seasons'. Snatches from the concertos floated out of the speakers. As 'Spring' turned into 'Summer', a pudgy man with a bald pate and large spectacles walked into the room. He was wearing a pair of baggy denims and a khaki safari shirt. He greeted Rishabhh, glanced at the still unopened case of earplugs, and smiled.

'Bravo! Bravo! You ride like the wind, and you choose not to use earplugs. A true automobile lover. My kind!' he said, as he applauded Rishabhh. He was joined by the man who had ushered us inside the mansion and a few other charlies who appeared to be house helps. Rishabhh was caught unawares by the sudden gush of unabashed admiration. He got up and bowed.

The man looked at a sheet of paper that was given to him by one of the house helps and shook his head in pleasant disbelief. 'Seven minutes, thirty-one seconds – amazing! My best was nine minutes, twenty-four seconds, on this same route you took up here, on a Ninja ZX9R. But that was when I was a lot younger, early 2000s. This is terrific. Bravo!'

I thought I had seen our host somewhere. He looked familiar, and I tried to build some sort of context into which I could place him. Rishabhh, too, looked as if he was trying to recall where he had seen the man. Our host walked up to the bar and picked out a bottle of Aberfeldy twenty-one-year-old. He held it up towards Rishabhh, who nodded. Rishabhh's gaze never left the man, from the time he poured the whisky into two chunky glasses to when he walked back towards him. As the man handed him his glass, I watched Rishabhh go numb with fear.

Our host chuckled.

'Don't worry, yaar. I'm Salim Ansari, or Petrol Salim – isn't that what the newspapers call me? Well, I am not as dangerous as I am made out to be. I have left those days far behind,' he said, as he sank into the couch and sipped his whisky.

Of course, it was Petrol Salim, the former don of Bombay! No wonder his face rang a bell. Salim was supposed to be an acclaimed automobile nut, which explained his interest in the Thruxton HT, and this was worrying. But we were faced with an even greater danger – what if Salim learnt Rishabhh was not as great a rider as he made himself out to be? What if he realized that Rishabhh's knowledge of automobiles was, at best, superficial? What would he do then? I stopped thinking, shut my eyes, and hoped Rishabhh would bluff like a master and deliver the performance of a lifetime.

'Sir, I can't believe I am sitting here with you. You once ruled Bombay. From what I've heard, you are one of the very few genuine automobile enthusiasts in India.'

Steepling his fingers and with his eyes shut, Petrol Salim smiled dismissively.

'The Don of Bombay, Salim the Sultan, Salim this, Salim that. The media has a way of hyping things. I was just doing what I grew up doing, but, you know, I really don't mind "Petrol Salim". It sounds good to this day.'

'If I may ask, sir, how did you come to be known by this name?'

Salim gazed beatifically into his glass of whisky and swirled it.

'Upwas Hotshot, one of my boys, he gave me that name. This was after we outmanoeuvred four police jeeps in a Dolphin. He said I had petrol running in my veins. "Bhai ke badan mein khoon nahin, petrol daudta hai!" This was in the early 1980s, but the name stuck,' said Salim. 'You are probably too young to have driven the Dolphin . . .'

'I've driven one! It could have done with more power, but I think it's fun to drive,' Rishabhh said.

'Exactly. Highly underpowered, notchy gear shifts but small and nimble, and quick around corners. I am pleased you know about it. Most young men these days just talk about Lamborghinis, Ferraris and McLarens.'

Rishabhh concurred with a modest nod and adroitly steered the topic away from the Sipani Dolphin. How had Salim grown to love cars? And where had he disappeared in the late 1990s after decades of making Bombay tremble with fear?

Petrol Salim was the second son of Ahmad Ansari, a car thief who stole big American cars in 1950s' and 1960s' Bombay. Ansari eventually made it big as the head of a gang of skilled car smugglers in the flashy 1970s and early 1980s. Back in the day, in pre-liberalization India, you knocked on Ansari's door if you didn't want a sad Hindustan Motors Ambassador or Fiat and were after something more technologically advanced. Rich car lovers across the country either chose from the cars Ansari had in stock, mostly Toyotas along with a few Mercedes-Benzes and BMWs, or placed orders for British automobiles such as Jaguars and Land Rovers. Ansari's men would then grease the palms of customs officers in Bombay or Madras, and the car would make its way to India, part by part. By the time he was twelve, Salim was already putting together powerful and exotic cars for his father's burgeoning clientele. At sixteen, two full years before he was eligible for a driving licence, he was even delivering cars, often in the dead of the night, to rich enthusiasts in Delhi and Ludhiana, among other cities. When he eventually took over the business, he not only built on his father's success, but also branched out. Salim smuggled gold and electronics into India and was among the first mafia bosses to both provide services to and extort money from Bombay's builders, who avariciously eyed prime real estate in a city surrounded by the sea. It is said that in the late 1980s he also financed a Bollywood movie. It was a typical boy-meets-girl love story, but the film flopped. According to critics, it was not just the lack of a plot and the twelve trashy songs that did the film in, the twenty-one random, inordinately long car and bike chase sequences had been too much to bear.

Over time Salim emerged as an elder statesman among the city's different mafia dons and often brokered peace between younger, brasher gangsters who were perhaps emblematic of a changing city. Old-timers still remembered him as the 'don of the dons'. Salim stayed away from dealing in drugs, never ignored an outstretched hand and always kept his word.

He was also known for his maniacal love for cars and motorcycles. He respected men who drove great cars and drove them well, and that respect extended to his enemies, too. The story goes that in his younger days he had once spared the life of a turncoat after witnessing his control over his motorcycle during a high-speed chase. Then, in the late 1990s, the last of the city's honourable dons all but disappeared. Where had he gone? Some said he had decamped to Dubai where he had legitimate businesses – shopping malls, electronic stores, theme parks, hotels – yet others said that he had been eliminated by the city's infamous 'encounter' cops in a top-secret operation. But nobody really knew. Had Petrol Salim simply got into a big red American car with a powerful Hemi engine and driven off into the sunset?

Salim lit a hand-rolled cigar, puffed and rotated it until he was satisfied with the evenness with which the open end of the cigar glowed. He blew the smoke out gently and gave a chuckle that crackled with phlegm. Did Rishabhh really think Petrol Salim would leave his beloved city and its roads on which the machines he had ridden and driven had left their tread marks? The potholed roads of Bombay, Salim told Rishabhh, were great teachers. He had learnt and refined his driving and riding skills on the city's roads and on the old winding highway up the mountains that led to Pune.

But there was a time when the heat of the extrajudicial killings conducted by the Bombay Police had gotten too much for even Petrol Salim. On the insistence of his children and wife, he headed to Dubai and returned after several years to a windswept cove at the foot of a hillock atop which he built his grand home. The mansion, said Salim, was accessible only by a private road, and many smooth palms had to be greased and were being greased to this day so that the former don would be left alone.

After his return to India, Salim was supposed to lie low for a year or two, but the spot he had chosen encouraged intense bouts of contemplation. The just king of Bombay never returned from his exile. He withdrew from the world of crime and, in the winter of his life, decided to focus all his energies on the one thing he had always wanted to do: build his own race car. The S1 was still a work in progress, but over time Salim had acquired many cars and motorcycles, both classic and contemporary, from a rare Invicta Black Prince to an Aprilia RSV Mille. Each morning he was at his happiest, tinkering with his cars and bikes. He restored abandoned vintage cars and motorcycles, and tweaked modern machines in an attempt to coax even more power out of them. And, when he achieved the latter objective, he drove them on the track that led up to his home. Designed by a famous Formula One expert, who was kidnapped in Monaco by Salim's men but rewarded generously for his efforts, the mini-track was inspired by the most challenging sections from the world's legendary Formula One circuits.

The series of successive corners Rishabhh had successfully attacked that day, each of them bumpy, and with a different angle, radius, length, inclination and shape, were, Salim told Rishabhh, modelled after vicious curves such as the Parabolica at Monza, the Loews Hairpin in Monaco, the Eau Rouge at Spa and the Brünnchen at Nürburgring.

'The seventh and the wickedest corner . . .' Salim fell silent. He removed his spectacles and cupped his eyes with his palm. I heard him sniffle.

'It has to be Tamburello. Ayrton Senna died while negotiating that one at Imola in 1994,' I told Rishabhh.

Rishabhh assumed a sombre expression and waited for the former mafia don to compose himself.

'Sir, the last corner, I've never come across a nastier one all my life. I felt it as soon as I entered it around 4300 rpm, but we all have our Tamburellos. The message I take from that tragedy is that we have to attack the twists and turns of our life with all we've got. We might not make it to the other side, but nobody can say we didn't try.'

Rishabhh was acing it. The bastard could have fooled me all over again.

Salim continued sniffling, but he nodded in agreement and flashed Rishabhh a thumbs up.

'God, it's been over two decades and I am still not over Senna's death. But I like what you said, we all have our Tamburellos. Yes, we do. But enough about me. Where did you learn to ride the way you do, Rishabhh?' asked Salim, wiping his tears and looking slightly sheepish.

Sitting there, in the lion's den, so to speak, Rishabhh reminisced about a childhood in Baroda, in which he coveted his neighbour's old Lambretta (Petrol Salim: 'Twin tone?' Rishabhh: 'Sir, red and white!'); hustling his father's Contessa on Baroda's narrow streets (Petrol Salim: 'The 1.8-litre 4ZB1 petrol engine was a smooth devil, wasn't it?' Rishabhh: 'Yes, very refined for that era!'); the tragedy that befell the Mehtaa household when the Contessa was stolen and never found (Petrol Salim: 'No! Do you want me to help you find it?'); the cars and motorcycles he had driven and ridden as a motoring journalist at *Turbo* (Rishabhh: 'A 911 across Austria, with the tail stepping out all the way!' PS: 'Woaaaaaaaahhhhhhhhhrrrrrrrr . . . Woohnnnnnn . . . wohaaarrrr . . . rrr'); a Ferrari 458 in Tuscany (PS: 'Telepathic feedback from the steering, eh?' Rishabhh: 'Mind reader, sir!'); a Yamaha R1 from Innsbruck to Berlin (Petrol Salim: 'Flat out? Germany has no speed limits! Love that country!' Rishabhh: 'We slingshotted into Berlin, sir, in about six hours. Ha!'); a recent outing in an old HM Ambassador (Petrol Salim: 'An Amby?' Rishabhh: 'Rear-wheel drive, sir. Great for drifting, total fun.'); and the Lexus LFA, a car he would do anything to get his hands on (Rishabhh: 'This is it, sir, nothing can beat the LFA when it comes to purity of design and purpose. Imagine a V10 in this day and age, and the noise it makes. It's amazing.')

He also spoke about his favourite car, apparently, a Saab 9-5.

'A 9-5? I always thought people like you would choose a Countach or an F40? Why a Saab?' asked Salim.

'I've driven the F40 and lusted after the Countach, but I'm big on turbochargers. I love the whole concept . . . I love little turbos and big turbos and superchargers . . . both the ones that help provide that initial boost and stuff like the ones on the 911 Turbo that rocket you into outer space . . . and I think nobody did turbochargers better than Saab,' Rishabhh said.

'Maybe you're right. You could do the usual stuff with cat-back exhausts, cold-air intakes and performance headers, but nothing like a spooling turbo for real grunt.'

'It's a pity that Saab is in ruins now. I can't believe the Chinese company that bought it is getting it to make electric cars!'

'Yes, yes, I'm aware of that. It is depressing. The whole electric car scene is depressing. But you're right. Turbocharging is something else. You know, Renault and its turbochargers changed the whole F1 game. It was a dangerous time, but also a very exciting one. What was that guy's name? He bunged a turbo into the RS01 . . .'

'Jean-Pierre Jabouille?'

'Yes, yes, Jabouille, 1979. What a season that was!' Salim walked towards the bar and refilled their glasses.

'You know, Rishabhh, we could spend a lot of time talking about cars. I haven't had this kind of chat in a long time. Some day I hope you and I can work together on my cars and bikes. Maybe we could tinker around with the turbocharger of one of my old Fords?'

'Sir, of course! Sir, I don't know how you will take this, but I think you should come back to Bombay and rule the city once again,' Rishabhh said. 'The city needs a great, noble don like you. There was Varadarajan

Mudaliar, and then there was you. We have no one like that today.'

A sad smile creased Salim's florid face.

'I belong to a different era, Rishabhh; that time is long gone. But yes, it would be nice to be back in the only city I've ever loved. But I don't know if now is the right time. The authorities were never able to arrest me all those years ago, but today I feel scared they will create trouble for me because of my religion. There are times when even I don't feel safe. Things are not as they once were, isn't it? Anyway, I don't think I should let my anxieties, imagined or otherwise, lead us away from the real reason why you are here. So, let's talk about the Thruxton HT,' said Salim, puffing heavily on his cigar.

Petrol Salim had first heard of the Velocette Venom Thruxton HT in the mid-1980s from a Turkish arms dealer named Ahmet. He was in Lebanon, and they had met and bonded over motorcycles.

'At the time, we both wanted Brough Superiors. And so we got talking, and discovered we both also loved Velocettes. I told him about this 1962 Venom Clubman that I was about to pick up, and he told me about his 1965 Venom MSS and the Thruxton he had had back in Istanbul. Ahmet had a fantastic collection, but he told me that there was this one bike he had been searching for – a bike that he would trade his entire collection for. And so, sitting there in an underground bunker in a bombed-out Beirut, both of us getting drunk on some excellent cognac, he told me about the Thruxton HT. I wonder why he told me about it. If I were in his place, I would have been very discreet.'

'How did Ahmet come to know about the existence of the Thruxton HT?' asked Rishabhh, echoing my own curiosity.

'Ah! It is an interesting tale. When he first told me about it, I thought he was pulling my leg. Later on, of course, everything made sense.'

In the late 1970s, Ahmet and his close friend, Altan, were riding towards Kuskoy, a small town nestled in the mountains off Turkey's Black Sea coast. Altan hailed from Kuskoy, which is famous for its whistled language. The people of Kuskoy, said Salim, used the famous whistled or 'bird' language to communicate with each other across the region's mountainous terrain. The two friends had stopped by a stream to take a break and smoke cigarettes as they closed in on Kuskoy, and that's when they heard someone whistle from high up in the mountains.

'Ahmet said Altan, who knew how to speak the

language, was surprised at the nature of the query. The person wanted to know how many motorcycles Ahmet possessed.

'"Tell him twenty-one," said Ahmet. "The very best."'

Altan relayed the answer across. The response was instantaneous: 'Your friend shouldn't be talking about motorcycles until he has ridden the Velocette Venom Thruxton HT.'

'And after that, there was just silence. Altan soon forgot about the incident, but it played on Ahmet's mind, and when he got back to Istanbul, he started to read up and ask around. And that led him to Birmingham. And, you know, he was hooked. He even went to Kuskoy several times, learnt to speak the whistled language – it's essentially Turkish, but you've got to know how to whistle it right – and spent many weekends riding around the mountains and shooting queries into the air. But there was no response. By the time I left Lebanon and got back to Bombay and did my own research, I was a madman. I visited England several times, met with Goodman and his family, and with some ex-Velocette staffers. Information was scarce, but from what little I heard of it, I knew I had to have it. Oh god, I've spent so many nights thinking about it!' Salim got up from the couch, refilled the whisky glasses and walked towards the large French windows.

Ahmet and Salim never met again after that night in Beirut, but they called each other once in a while and kept tabs on what the other was doing.

'Both of us were curious about how the other's quest for the motorcycle and Chowfin Singh was coming along. We sent our people out into the world, hunting for the bike in every nook and cranny. His people kept a watch on my people, and my people informed me about what his people were doing. About two months ago, he contacted me. He said he had gotten a call. The caller, who spoke in the whistled language, told him, "It's getting close. Are you ready?" Ahmet wanted to know where the motorcycle was. The caller gave him approximate details, and the line went dead. But Ahmet was in no state to ride. He was dying of cancer. But he told me that after a lot of thinking, he had decided he would entrust the secret to me. He said he thought that a bike like that needed a man and a rider like me, someone who had been relentlessly searching for it for almost as long as he had. Ahmet died a week after our conversation, and here I am, a couple of steps away, I think, from achieving a lifelong ambition.'

'Sir, if I were you, I'd be out riding the Thruxton …'

Salim looked at the floor and nodded slowly.

'There is a time for everything but at the same time, Rishabhh, we have so little of it. I wish I had had this opportunity when I was in my prime, when I was insanely quick. Petrol Salim, even twenty years ago, would have been a match for the Thruxton HT. Now, I'm not so sure. My lap times have been depressing. My reflexes aren't quite the same. I don't corner as hard as I once did, I brake too early, I make too many mistakes. I'm afraid that's what it is. For the first time in his life, Petrol Salim is wary of getting astride a motorcycle. I don't think I'm up to the challenge. And so . . .'

Salim took off his spectacles and wiped the lens with the hem of his shirt. He placed them firmly back on his nose and looked at Rishabhh.

'Ever since Ahmet died, I've been searching for someone who can do justice to the Thruxton HT. I'm not looking for someone who can just ride fast, no, I want someone who embodies the spirit of motorcycling. When I came across your article, I knew it had to be you. You actually saw the HT and Chowfin Singh – they revealed themselves to you! Your passion for cars and bikes shines through in the way you write, talk and ride. The HT, of course, is not in this world that you and I inhabit. It is elsewhere.

But, who knows, you could just be the one capable enough of hunting it down and riding it.'

'Oh, thank you, sir. I just–'

'An occasion like this needs to be celebrated.'

Salim asked his house helps to get him a bottle of Dom Perignon.

'I won't disagree, but, if you don't mind my asking, how did you get me out of that place? Where was I? Who were those guys?'

The don chuckled.

'Kartar and company. They owed me a few favours,' he said, as he uncorked the bottle of Dom Perignon and poured the champagne into the flutes.

'I read that great article of yours pretty late. By then, you were already on the Grand Trunk Road. And then my men reported that you were last seen in Gangtok. I combed Sikkim, but I realized you could be elsewhere or, since this is the Thruxton HT we are talking about, anywhere. So, I got in touch with all the powerful people I knew – from the past, the present and the future. And even those men who live inside people's heads. Kartar was one of them.'

'I'm afraid I'm confused.'

'You see,' Salim said, rising slowly from the couch like a mushroom cloud, 'Kartar and the other overlords of Bombay you met were characters in a low-budget

Hindi movie that was released in the early 1970s, I think. It had a few unknown actors and the movie flopped, but I don't know why, some people loved it, like the gentleman whose head Kartar and the others were stuck in. I suppose the characters really made an impression on him – for their audacity, their chutzpah, their style, whatever. And inside his head, they continued their activities, just like in the movie. Gunrunning, smuggling, extortion, all that. As Kartar told me, they were creatures of the imagination and memory, but they were alive, and they were kings of a city, even if it was only in someone's head. I know it sounds crazy, but that's how it is. Anyway, in the movie, Inspector Vijay ends up defeating these bad men. This entire movie kept playing in a loop, like a programme that's always running in the background on your phone or your computer. Kartar and his friends wanted that to end. To Kartar, Inspector Vijay represented not only an enemy but also Bollywood's hackneyed way of looking at things. Good triumphs over evil, truth always wins, that sort of thing. That's not how it always works, right? So, they got in touch with me.'

'And you bumped Inspector Vijay off?'

'Oh no, no.' Salim laughed. 'I just got him transferred out of Bombay.'

'Salim sir, I think I'll faint right now, but let me

get this straight: some guy watched a movie fifty years ago and liked it. He must have remembered it often, especially these particular characters. And you got Inspector Vijay, the hero of the movie, transferred to another city? And all of this happened inside this gentleman's head? You altered someone's memory! How did you do that?'

Salim rubbed his nose and smiled.

'Let's just say that it was an unusual request. I found it pretty amusing. It was a bit more complicated than the usual requests I got back when I was in Bombay, but that great city teaches you how to get things done. Once you've figured out Bombay, everything else is just, you know . . . I've always believed that we should do what we can.'

'I don't know what to say, sir, but hell, you are a king among men,' said Rishabhh. And he was right.

This guy, not me, was god, I thought. He could do just about anything.

The short, slight man who had welcomed us inside the mansion walked into the room and whispered into Salim's ear.

'Ah, yes, yes, I'll be done soon. Ask him to wait,' Salim said, and then he turned to Rishabhh.

'So, Rishabhh, I'm glad we met. It's been great

fun chatting with you, and we should really go riding together.'

'Of course, sir.'

'Good, good. But let's get back to the reason you are here – you see, you've ticked all my boxes. But I think I need to be doubly sure, separate the wheat from the chaff. Since Ahmet has bestowed this great responsibility on me – and I'm doing this without his consent – it's the least I think I can do. You know, if there's one thing I hate, it's these pseudo-enthusiasts who strut around thinking they know everything there is to know about the automobile or motorcycle–'

'Tell me about it,' Rishabhh said.

'Right, so how do I put it, let's have a little test to gauge how good a motorcyclist you really are. I'll be asking you five questions about motorcycles. Consider this your own Tamburello. If you succeed, you could get to ride the Thruxton; if you don't, well . . .' Salim picked up the earplugs case lying on the table and snapped it in a theatrical manner.

Rishabhh sat upright on the couch. I could hear him call out my name silently. I felt sorry for the bastard. This was not Rishabhh's Tamburello, it was mine. I told Rishabhh to go for it.

'Game on, sir,' said Rishabhh.

'Excellent! Let's do some Moto-Quizzing!' Salim said, rubbing his hands in glee. He called out for one of his man Fridays, who entered the room with an Apple iPad. As Salim tapped on his iPad, two other men walked in. One of them carried a trumpet and the other hand cymbals, and they took up positions behind Rishabhh.

Motorized shades dropped over the windows in the room. It was now cooler than before. Two pools of light fell on Salim and Rishabhh from niches in the ceiling.

'Are you ready? Okay, here we go, you have thirty seconds to answer each question.'

Salim read out the first question from his iPad.

'Which was the first Japanese production motorcycle to feature a forkless front suspension?'

'Of course, it is the . . .' Rishabhh said, fingertips on his temples, simulating deep thought.

The names of several motorbikes flashed in my head. I knew it was not a Suzuki, and definitely not a Honda. That meant . . .

'Yamaha GTS1000!' Rishabhh said and sat back with an air of nonchalance.

'Bravo!' Salim nodded at the two men who stood behind him. The trumpet blared and the cymbals clashed.

'Which 1969 motorcycle was introduced in a paint scheme similar to the Shelby Mustang Cobra of the same era?'

'Kawasaki Mach III.'

The trumpet blared . . .

'Kya baat hai! Two out of two. Interesting. Okay, what is a valve overlap?'

'On the exhaust stroke, the intake and exhaust valve are open at the same time for a few degrees around the top dead centre. This is called a valve overlap,' Rishabhh said, repeating my answer verbatim.

This time the trumpeter allowed the cymbals to clash first.

'Good. Two more left.' Salim beamed at Rishabhh.

'Which company built the 1962 Super Lassie? I have one in my garage.'

Salim drew the iPad to his chest and waited for Rishabhh's answer.

'Pointer,' Rishabhh said a trifle dismissively, and put one leg over the other.

Salim got up from the couch and looked admiringly at Rishabhh. He put the iPad away and walked across the room.

'Okay, I know this will be highly subjective,' he said, 'but which, according to you, are the three most significant production motorcycles of all time and why? You can take your time with this. Some more champagne?'

Rishabhh nodded and waited for my cue. I walked over to the window and thought of a rainy night many years ago. Madhavi had left that morning for her brother's home after yet another showdown provoked by Koman's alcoholism, and we were sitting in the veranda of his home chatting about this motorcycle and that motorcycle.

Somewhere along the way, like folks who love motorcycles are wont to do, especially folks whose means never match up to their enthusiasm, we decided, for the umpteenth time in our lives, to hypothetically populate our garage with the best machines ever made.

Our previous attempts at achieving some sort of a consensus on the choice of machines had always fallen flat. We had always scoffed at each other's choices, assailing each other with a fusillade of technical specifications, prejudices and unwavering opinions about the motorcycles we discussed.

That night, though, after debating for over two hours, we found ourselves on the same page. The machines we 'parked in the garage' that night were the 1948 Vincent Black Shadow, because of its massive impact on motorcycle design; the 1950 Norton Manx, because its 'featherbed' chassis has been copied by every motorcycle maker since; and the 1994 Ducati 916, because a motorcycle more beautiful than this Duc was yet to be made (and that still holds true, if you ask me). If these were good enough for Koman and me, they would be good enough for Petrol Salim, too, I thought, and walked over to Rishabhh.

Salim shut his eyes and nodded as Rishabhh, with suitable emphasis and drama, told him about his all-time favourite motorcycles. When the don opened his eyes, I noticed that they had welled up. He walked towards Rishabhh, arms outstretched and embraced him.

'I own two of these motorcycles you just spoke about. I don't know whether I'd pick the Duc, maybe, a CB750, or a GSX-R750, the original one, but I'm impressed all the same. You are the man. *You are the man*,' he said.

His man Friday started applauding, and he was joined by the house helps. The applause continued for a long time, interspersed with the clash of cymbals and the blare of the trumpet. When it died down, Salim refilled Rishabhh's glass, and the two men sat down.

'Now, about the Thruxton HT. So, here's what

Ahmet told me, "You have to look for it where everyone's search ends." So, what is that place where you begin your search?'

I nearly fell off the couch. Ahmet had echoed Bun Babu's advice.

'I'm all ears, sir,' said Rishabhh.

'The place is G-o-o-o-o-o-o-o-o-o-g-l-e,' said Salim, stretching out the first consonant a mile. 'I don't think Ahmet was the kind who'd prank someone just before dying, but yes, *Google*, that's what he said, and that's what you've got to work with. I'd advise you to act on it right away, because, apparently, this is the best chance anyone will have of getting close to the Thruxton HT.'

And with that, he got up, wished Rishabhh luck and walked out of the room. A few minutes later, the chauffeur appeared and indicated that it was time for Rishabhh to leave.

14

'So?' I said, as we entered Rishabhh's apartment. Rishabhh was relieved to discover that barely three days had passed since we, well, dropped down from Gangtok, and that no one at his magazine seemed to have noticed the absence of his tweets on their Twitter timeline. But there was work to be done.

'So?' he said. 'So, the first thing you are going to do is write ten posts on those fucking British bikes and a 4,000-word article on our journey till Rajgir. I'll figure out the rest. And you better not try and blackmail me again – this time I won't care. Because if I do it one more time, I'd be sure I'm going mad. I should be at the shrink's right now!'

'Okay,' I said.

'And I want those posts by tomorrow morning!' Rishabhh slammed his bedroom door shut.

I decided to leave Rishabhh alone for the time being and booted up the desktop at his apartment. A lot had happened. Or perhaps nothing had happened. Or, it had all happened inside our heads. And the answer was apparently Google. Nonsense!

I looked at the blank document on the computer screen, and, as most writers are wont to do, decided to check email and Facebook before getting down to work on the articles Rishabhh needed. Google's home page stared back at me from the computer screen. 'Just what did Petrol Salim mean when he said Google was the answer?' I thought to myself and reflexively typed 'Velocette' into the search bar.

The search engine delivered 2,020,000 results, an ocean of information on Velocette, the Venom and the Thruxton, and all manner of vintage and classic British motorcycles.

I was familiar with these waters. I knew all about the sites, the videos and the forums Google would throw up on being queried about 'Velocette' (or even 'Chowfin Singh', 'British motorcycle racing', 'Thruxton HT' and some ten other parameters). I was walking down the same road I had walked all these years in the hope that I would perhaps see something new that day. Nothing of the sort happened, of course, but, as always, I was drawn to sites owned by Velocette

Venom owners in England and elsewhere; to the *Classic Bike* magazine's online edition in which I read an article about the blindly ambitious, and yet today alluringly rare, Hesketh V1000 from the 1980s, the golden days of British drag racing; and to numerous other forums on which I, despite resisting the urge, offered my two bits. I advised some people on how to remanufacture push rods for the Venom engine and informed some others that a 1.5 inch GP carb, larger valves and hotter cams on a 580cc Thruxton would only work if one beefed up the drive side of the custom cast crankcase to keep the crank from flexing because of the extra grunt.

Rishabhh walked into the kitchen a little past midnight and emerged with a bottle of water.

'Hello, I hope you have begun work on those posts. Tomorrow morning . . .' he said.

I assured him that I was on it.

He grumbled and lit a cigarette.

'Petrol Salim has put on so much weight, right?' he said and sniggered.

'Yes, he shouldn't be riding sports bikes; I don't think fat people should be allowed to ride bikes,' I said, and hurriedly added, 'Not that I'm calling you fat.'

'Of course, I'm not, I've only got a slight paunch and I'm not as large as Petrol Salim,' he said defensively.

'Google, it seems. That's what he said, didn't he? As if no one knew about Google in the first place.'

My brain rewound to the last few minutes we spent inside Salim's mansion. The gangster hadn't simply said 'Google' the way a normal person would. The revelation that had emerged, like a party horn, from Salim's mouth was a prolonged guttural incantation: 'G-o-o-o-o-o-o-o-o-o-gle'. Was that guy hinting at something? Did that mean we would have to journey to the outer reaches of the Internet to find the Thruxton HT? Were we supposed to begin our search, as Bun Babu had told us, where others ended theirs? How deep do you plunge into Google in search of something or someone? I haven't ever gone beyond twenty-odd pages. I have either found what I was looking for, or, as was the case with the Thruxton HT, abandoned my search after repeatedly encountering results that had nothing to do with the motorcycle per se. Do the truly passionate go way further?

I waited for Rishabhh to settle into his bed, and then hit Google again. I relentlessly bounded across the 'Os' of the search engine until I arrived at what I took to be the desolate outer periphery of the world of Velocette, as archived, recorded and updated by Google. It was a lifeless land of broken links and dry databases. The name 'Velocette' was a faint echo in the catalogues of dealers of spare parts and in the frozen chatter on message boards and forums. But I carried on resolutely.

As I landed on the twenty-second page of the search results, I thought I heard something approaching from afar. It sounded like a rogue wave. I got up from the chair and looked out of the window, but realized that the noise was emanating from the left corner of the computer screen. I checked the speakers and ascertained that they were switched off, and also checked if I hadn't inadvertently clicked on any motorcycle advertisements while surfing the results on Google. The aural speck was growing rapidly. The nature of the noise was also more discernible now. It was a motorcycle, being ridden at full tilt. High rpm stuff, probably around 9800. I sat up.

One of my favourite pastimes, regardless of whether I am lying on the boundary wall of Azhakappadath house, or strolling on the streets of Milan or London, is to decode the make of an approaching motorcycle from the nature and texture of its exhaust note. At times like these I shut my eyes and see with my ears, and I'm delighted if the motorcycle that eventually flies past me corresponds to the aural image I have of it. India, and that includes Bombay, Delhi, Bangalore and Kollengode, doesn't pose much of a challenge, since most of the motorcycles that are ridden in our country are single-cylinder bikes: Bajaj Pulsars, KTMs, Enfields, the occasional two-stroke Jawa and so on. Europe, of course, is markedly different and more challenging. With everything from large singles to inline-fours and V4s and at times even inline six-cylinder motorcycles, it is a continent of tonal richness and diversity.

But the noise that emerged from the computer screen was unlike anything I had heard before. It was crisp, like a two-stroke motorcycle, but at times it also rumbled like a V-twin. By the time it streaked past me, the exhaust note had turned into an eerie wail. What was it? A Honda CBX? A Ducati Panigale? A six-cylinder boxer? Or, was it the Thruxton itself?

I heard the screech of tyres. The motorcycle idled before revving impatiently, almost as if it was waiting for me to catch up with it. Was it leading me somewhere? I decided to give chase and clicked on the next 'O' of Google. As if on cue, I heard the motorcycle accelerating away, and by the time I was on the next page, it was waiting for me to come chasing after it again.

The sequence repeated itself across the remaining pages of Google's search results until we came to the thirty-ninth and last page. This time, instead of the restless revving, there was silence. I heard a voice. It was indistinct but whoever it was, he seemed to be expressing his disapproval at something in an affectionate manner. The motorcycle growled, and everything went quiet inside the computer.

Rishabhh burst into the drawing room.

'What the fuck is happening here, dude? I've been hearing some strange shit. Are you there?'

'Hello . . . hello?'

Someone greeted us from inside the computer. He had a shrill voice, and he sounded both curious and expectant.

The man called out to us again. This time I responded to his greeting.

'Hello! Is that Chowfin Singh?'

'That's right! And gentlemen, who are you?'

15

Chowfin Singh and I had spoken for barely an hour, but it seemed as if we had known each other for years. We were both true motorcyclists who had ridden long and hard, and we had tales to tell.

Chowfin was warm and humble, though his voice – he sounded like a screechy bicycle brake each time he opened his mouth – was something else.

I had quickly summarized the route we had taken to get to him. That included gently breaking the news of the car crash that wiped out his family in the early 1970s – it was met with a stoic silence – and getting him to try and grasp the concept of the Internet inside which he was, for all practical purposes, located at the time. Now, it was his turn to tell us where he'd been riding all these years.

Chowfin laughed. 'I never thought I'd meet

someone who I could tell this to. Maybe Peter, but he . . . is not around any more. You tell me, KK, who would ever believe the story of a prototype motorcycle that went rogue?' he said.

'A little god from a little village in Kerala who's been searching for that very bike!' I said, and we all laughed, including, surprisingly, Rishabhh who sat at a safe distance from the computer.

'You know, KK, sometimes I think these stories, what you just told me, what I'm going to tell you now, these are not our stories. Maybe my motorcycle here is scripting all of it. Maybe this is her story . . .'

The first thing that crossed Chowfin Singh's mind as he looked at that ungainly but defiant motorcycle in Birmingham all those years ago was a massive burnout.

'I wanted to peel those tyres off!'

'And then you should have headed out, looking for Honda and Kawasaki riders, and rubbed their noses to the ground,' I said. Chowfin chortled, sounding like a clattering of jackdaws. As he walked towards it, Chowfin was aware that the ride would be no ordinary one, but even the most fervid of his dreams, he told us, paled before the thrilling insanity that was triggered the moment he got astride the HT and reined it in.

'I don't know what really happened after we took

off from the test track. I remember seeing a terrified Vesely, I remember laughing hard. After that, it is all a blur.'

'Zero to hundred in, like what, half a second?' I said, sounding like an obsessive, speed-crazy maniac.

'I don't know! The Velo's speedometer never worked. It still doesn't. I don't quite know how powerful she is, whether it's 70 bhp or 50,000 bhp. All I can say is we are invisible to the naked eye and to any sort of radar technology. It took me days to get used to the false neutrals and the vibrations, months to get used to just the throttle response and the pace. I still haven't gotten used to how quick she can be. It was many months before I could confidently lean her into corners. But we kept riding and riding and riding. Across mountains and deserts, over oceans and cities and villages and countries. We were this . . . this harsh strip of sound that roamed the earth . . .

'I don't know how long we kept riding, but it must have been around a year or more. I say this because after many, many months we slowed down just a touch, and I started riding normally, and by that, I mean on regular roads and at street-legal speeds. I didn't know where we had landed, or where she was taking me, but soon the road signs made it clear – we were in Germany, and we were headed to Nürburgring.'

'The Ring!' I cried. 'This must have been around April 1972. Were you headed for the races? The MotoGP? Of course, back then it was called the FIM Motorcycle Grand Prix World Championship. The change of name happened in 1978.'

'Yes, the Motorcycle Grand Prix.'

'1972 was a great season. Ago must have been there, and Granath, and Newcombe . . .'

'Yes, yes. You know, I might have modelled my riding style after Mike Hailwood, but Agostini was my hero.'

'I loved Hailwood. Did you watch all the races? Agostini won the championship that year, didn't he?'

'He did, or maybe he didn't.' An impish laugh shot out of the computer screen.

'No, don't tell me! Oh my god!'

I nearly died when I heard what Chowfin and the HT had done. Here, in a nutshell, is what happened on the last Sunday of April of 1972, and every Motorcycle Grand Prix Sunday that year.

On that April afternoon, Chowfin Singh rode towards the circuit to compete against Agostini and his MV Agusta, and against various other riders and their steeds, which were among the best racing motorcycles of the time. The MotoGP season of 1972 was a hard-fought one, but though the 500cc class, in which Chowfin competed, had some world-class riders, it was dominated by a handsome Italian named Giacomo Agostini.

Agostini, who also raced 350cc motorcycles, won fifteen world championship titles and 122 Grand Prix between the years 1964 and 1976. In 1972, as with the previous years, he and the MV Agusta were considered unbeatable. The record shows that Ago was crowned the world champion that year, but now is as good a time as any to set it straight.

'I knew what the HT was capable of, and in the spirit of fairness, I decided to give the guys a head start of about five laps. We hung around at a fair distance from the track, and then, about fifteen minutes after the race started, I just blasted into it.'

But the going wasn't easy for Chowfin Singh. He was nervous and impatient, and unable to control the motorcycle's tremendous pace. With the kind of speeds the HT was doing, Chowfin said, they would constantly overshoot the track and be propelled into the skies, and would then have to turn around to launch another assault.

'I was merely hanging on to the bike. It was clear to me that she wanted to annihilate the opposition and wouldn't ever slow down,' said Chowfin. 'It was one thing to streak across the skies and blast across deserts and quite another to try and harness the HT's power in a closed environment such as a race track. Basically, I think I couldn't handle the pressure.'

'Lack of race cred. Happens,' I said in a sparkling display of fatuity. The champion rider let that pass, and told us what happened next.

'Just when I thought our first ever proper race would end disastrously, the Velo slowed down a touch. She became more reasonable, less wilful. I knew then that if I managed to point her in the right direction, we still had a good chance of winning the race.'

Within the next ten minutes, Chowfin took out Yamaha's Lothar, Kawasaki's Araoka, Honda's Nelson, and Granath and Newcombe in no time at all. And then he got Alberto Pagani.

'Crazy! So, now it was just the hunter and the hunted. Giacomo Agostini versus Chowfin Singh. What a feeling that must have been,' I said, moving closer to the computer screen.

'Yes! But Ago was quick! The god of motorcycle racing. He was nearly as quick as I was.'

Agostini, attired in trademark red-and-white leathers, was riding a perfectly set-up racing machine, and Chowfin said he knew how to extract every ounce of the stupendous power it delivered. With his fluid riding style, he made short work of the track's tricky corners and ripped across it like a bullet.

Chowfin gained on the Italian several times, but he was never able to pass Agostini.

Then came the turning point. 'Up ahead was Ago, leading by about hundred metres. I knew Bergwerk was coming up. When it did, Ago slowed down and braked. We didn't. We took Bergwerk flat out. Just like that!'

'You took Bergwerk flat out? Bergwerk. Flat. Out. What a guy!'

I sat back and sighed. Bergwerk was a man-eater, Nürburgring's most vicious corner. Many talented racers have been felled by the combination of a tight right-hand corner, followed immediately by a left hand kink that crowns a crest on the track. How had this man attacked a wicked bend at that speed? To negotiate a turn or a curve on a road, or a racing track, a motorcyclist, a driver, or a cyclist has to slow down, brake at an ideal point and then accelerate their way out of it once they reach the apex or the inner edge of the corner.

Some people did it better and faster than others, but the fundamental rule still applied. That was what Koman had taught me all those years ago up in the hills surrounding Kollengode, and that was what everyone did, from the current MotoGP legend Valentino Rossi to punks on 100cc two-stroke bikes. Chowfin's calculated, precise and rapid assault on Bergwerk was a stupendous feat, the likes of which had never been attempted before. On that April Sunday, as Agostini cautiously tackled Bergwerk, his opponent sped past, converting the gain of a few seconds into an unassailable lead. That margin between the two riders kept widening as the race progressed. Agostini finished the race in an hour and some seven minutes. But by that time, an elated Chowfin had lapped him over five times, and was already on his way to Clermont-Ferrand where he awaited yet another duel with the champ.

By the end of the season, the Thruxton HT had accomplished two objectives: it had helped Chowfin Singh transform himself from a tearaway motorcyclist into a skilful racer, and it had decimated all manner of Italian, German and Japanese opposition.

It had nothing left to prove to itself, at least on earth. At the end of the last race in Spain, the Thruxton HT once again took off with its rider towards the skies. This time it didn't stop until it had launched itself and its rider into orbit.

'The wind chill must have been crazy up there,' I said.

'Oh yes, it does get pretty cold, but it's a great place to perfect your cornering skills.'

'Yeah? How does that work?'

'I don't know the actual science behind it, but I tried a hundred different orbits, after accounting for, you know, the pull of gravity, the way everything just keeps rotating, the moon and the earth and all.'

'So, different entry speeds, lean angles, entry and exit points?'

'Yes! And if you want to ever blast away from the earth, the ideal apex is somewhere near the North Pole, say, twenty degrees below it. If it's a clear day, all the better. I must have done it thousands of times.'

'But what did you . . . I mean I'm just asking, the stock HT did all this? Did you bump up compression, fit bigger carburettors and all? Polished manifolds and heads and bigger valves would have helped, right?'

'No, no, no, nothing. The Velo's completely stock. No modifications. But you're right. Sometimes even I wondered how she'd cope with the frigidity up there, but no problems at all. Not even when we roamed around deep space, chasing comets and all.'

'Hell!'

'Yeah, that was good fun. We raced a couple of

comets. They are very quick and they spray a lot of debris around so it's tough to stay in their slipstream.'

'Magnificent, sir, magnificent. Did you, by any chance, encounter black holes and stuff?' Rishabhh asked.

'Just two. At least I think they were black holes. The last one got me here, into this place, but it was peaceful compared to the first one. Everything, sort of, juddered. I had to stand up on the pegs and ride like I was on a trail. I had to use the front brake a lot. I don't remember much of it. Everything comes at you at some 10,000 kph. And absolutely no reference points, you know what I mean?'

'Fucking hell!' I said.

'It was tricky, but I thought I modulated the throttle well. That is the trick, I suppose, to escape a black hole on a capable motorcycle. Never stop completely, just keep moving. Move fast, faster than what's sucking you in.'

'That must have been the high point of your amazing ride,' I said.

'No, not really. The high point was what happened after I exited the first black hole.'

When he rode out of the first black hole, Chowfin found himself in a familiar place – at the edge of the solar system. This time, though, he was not alone.

'After such a long time with the Velo, I thought nothing would surprise me. But they were all there, my heroes, somewhere near Pluto. Saarinen on his Yamaha, Sheene and his Suzuki, Hailwood on his Honda and a couple of other chaps I couldn't place. It's true, great motorcyclists never die, they simply find another place to ride.'

My eyes welled up. Jarno Saarinen, Mike 'The Bike' Hailwood, and Barry Sheene were not just Chowfin's heroes, they were my idols, too. Saarinen was barely twenty-eight when he died in a tragic crash at Monza in 1973. Had he lived longer, the 'Baron' would have, I'm pretty certain, given Agostini a tough time. And Hailwood and Sheene! Such natural riders. Who can forget Hailwood's incredible comeback at the Isle of Man in 1978?

Defeating Agostini and his world-beating MV Agusta had obviously not been enough for the Thruxton HT. It was determined to prove its supremacy over all manner of opposition, across time and space. It had bided its time and waited for one of the greatest assemblage of riders in history before returning to the edge of the solar system from somewhere deep in space to take part in the mad dash from Pluto to Mercury, a no-holds-barred zigzag across the planets.

When Chowfin Singh arrived near Pluto, he saw

the riders lined up, bobbing noiselessly in the immense vacuum of space. Hailwood and Saarinen occupied the first two positions, followed by Sheene. Chowfin was last on the grid. He saw Hailwood look around impatiently and waved out to him. His enthusiastic overture was acknowledged with a nod. Chowfin felt thrilled. In the distance, a star imploded upon itself in a blaze of green. The race had begun. Hailwood and Saarinen blasted off, followed closely by Sheene. Chowfin wrung the Thruxton HT's throttle open and by the time they neared Neptune, he had moved up to the fifth position.

'Must have been almost like a slalom course up in the heavens, eh?' I said.

'Yes, but, KK, wherever you are in the universe, the basic lessons of riding fast still hold. Look ahead, keep the revs around half mast, don't turn in too early, and run wide around bends, you know.'

'That's true.'

'Neptune and Uranus were peaceful compared to Saturn, but the rings around Saturn were madness. Just too many asteroids, and too much dust; you had to keep making a million corrections as you rode.'

'Mid-corner corrections are the worst.'

By the time Chowfin exited Saturn, he had moved

further up the field and was now placed fourth, behind Hailwood, Saarinen and Sheene. The three men ahead of him were quicker around the shroud of cold clouds that cover the outer planets of the solar system. Chowfin, though, didn't lose hope and never lost sight of Sheene, who was hanging off his motorcycle, just as he used to back on earth. But Sheene appeared to slow down as Jupiter swung into view.

'I couldn't believe my luck. Barry Sheene's Suzuki had blown a head gasket!' said Chowfin.

'Imagine, a Suzuki blowing its gasket! I thought these Japanese were obsessed with reliability.' I cackled, reiterating my indifference to the allure of Japanese motorcycles.

'Give them tender loving care and British bikes are the best.'

'Absolutely!'

Chowfin made the most of Barry Sheene's rotten luck. He swept out of Jupiter's orbit and went after Saarinen.

'That chase was amazing. Imagine this: Saarinen and I, we were approaching Mars, and saw a huge dust storm covering the entire planet. We darted around each other; we could barely see anything, but when I finally emerged out of the storm and blasted around Mars, I knew I had left him behind. And my hopes lifted further when I saw the earth in the distance.'

Hailwood was still the leader by a comfortable margin, and the doughty rider looked set to increase the gap. The Brit downshifted, and slowed down as he approached the earth, aiming for the best possible exit route out of the planet's orbit. Chowfin, though, didn't have to slow down. He knew the contours of the earth like nobody did. He also knew this was the best chance he would get to overtake Hailwood. He aimed for his favourite spot, 'some twenty degrees below the North Pole', and leaned in as hard as he ever had. Both the Thruxton and its rider held their nerve as they doggedly broke out of the planet's gravitational pull and shot out wide.

Chowfin's audacious move stunned Hailwood, who, nevertheless, gave chase. But it was too late. He probably watched with despair as Chowfin swam around Venus, tore ahead towards Mercury and hung off his motorcycle as he swooshed by the planet closest to the sun.

The Thruxton reared up in triumph. Chowfin pumped his fist in the dense, hot air. Behind him the sun shone bright and the nine planets of the solar system orbited around him.

'Just like your birthmark!' I said.

Chowfin smiled. I could tell he was slightly embarrassed. 'That, well, I don't know. But my grandmother would have been proud. She always said I was destined for great things, that I was a child of the universe. But aren't all grandmothers like that?'

'Not just your grandmother, I think diehard motorcyclists everywhere would be proud of you, Chowfin Singh. Yours has been the ultimate ride,' I said.

'Mr Singh, tell me, you're a well-travelled man, so have you ever come across purple slugs?'

'Uhhhh . . . no, no purple slugs, but I saw many wondrous things . . . I can't even begin to describe half of them. But maybe now it's somebody else's turn to see them. If that's what the Velo wants, that is what will happen.'

'The motorcycle is doing all this, you mean?' Rishabhh was sprawled on his beanbag, blowing sceptical smoke rings into the air.

'I have often thought about it all these years. What made her behave that way all those years ago? Why did she take me on this wild ride? Where do you and KK fit into this?'

Chowfin Singh attempted to answer his own questions with even more questions. Had the Thruxton

HT escaped from Birmingham some fifty years ago because it didn't want to be known forever as the ugly motorcycle that brought Velocette down? Had it chosen and transformed him from a rookie rider into an accomplished motorcyclist just so that Chowfin could help it vanquish every other motorcycle in the world? Did the Thruxton HT engineer an eruption of motorcycle madness in me? Was it the Thruxton HT that made Rishabhh conjure up an imaginary ending to his story on Varanasi? And . . . was I the chosen one?

'Maybe she has decided it is time for the world to know about her: the greatest British motorcycle that was ever built, a champion of champions. Perhaps, it will happen through this article you will write. I don't know . . .' Chowfin trailed off.

I felt coyly proud and smiled.

'Well, I hope I get to ride the HT. I've waited for too long, and I can only hope the great motorcycle finds me worthy enough. What else can I say?' I said, in a voluble display of anxiety.

That's when the doorbell rang.

16

Who was it at this hour, I wondered. It was nearing three in the night. I looked at Rishabhh who peered timidly at the door. The doorbell rang again. This time Rishabhh let out a volley of expletives and marched towards the door.

I heard the door being opened and slammed shut the next instant. As Rishabhh streaked silently into the bedroom, I heard two violent thuds – someone was trying to ram the door open. I heard another thud, and then the multi-levered lock snapped open. Alarmed, I rushed towards the door and was greeted by an extraordinary sight: three muscular, long-haired blond men were striding into the apartment. They wore iron helmets with nasal helms and carried battleaxes. I was so scared I scampered under the sofa. With their coarse woollen tunics and crude leather boots, they looked like Vikings set for battle. But what were they doing here? Two of them headed towards the bedroom, while the tallest and broadest among them, a man with a regal mien, stared impassively at the computer. His followers smashed open the bedroom door and dragged a whimpering Rishabhh from under the bed.

I shouted at them and at the Viking from under the sofa. From inside the Internet, a concerned Chowfin Singh's shrill enquiry about our well-being added an unbearable dimension to the general pandemonium.

The two lackeys deposited Rishabhh at the feet of their leader. The man looked at Rishabhh and then picked him up, the way you or I would pick up a loaf of bread or a book, and secured him in the crook of his right arm. Rishabhh croaked repeatedly and flailed about, until a hard whack from one of the other Vikings shut him up. The leader of the group grunted at his men, who in turn lifted the sofa and plucked me up and handed me over to their leader. What the fuck, I thought, how could these bastards see me? When had I turned tactile? And what did I look like, by the way? But anyway, there we were, both Rishabhh and I, ensconced in the crook of the arms of a massive Viking.

The big Viking grunted again, upon which one of

his men walked up to the computer. He fiddled with the trackpad of Rishabhh's laptop, turned around and nodded at his leader. A few seconds later, a guttural incantation filled the room, and it came from the mouth of the big Viking. He continued chanting until the grating noise hung heavy around us. I saw him open his blue eyes and stare at the computer.

At first I thought I was imagining things, but then I looked closely and saw that the pupils of his eyes were no longer circular, they had taken a familiar shape: two triangles with tails, or something like that.

'KK, Rishabhh! What is happening? Are you both fine?' It was Chowfin again, understandably so.

'Chowfin, we're good. I think . . . I have a feeling we're being transported inside the Internet. Sort of like Bluetooth,' I said.

'What? What does that mean? Are you okay? Hello?'

And indeed, I was right. The pupils of the Viking's eyes had taken the shape of the Bluetooth logo! Was he *Bluetooth* himself? The legendary Viking king after whom the technology was named, whatever his real name was. I'd read about this guy, but I couldn't recall his real name. I kept staring at his face, enduring the unique agony of a tip-of-the-tongue experience until Bluetooth's eyes started flashing, and he let go of us.

Rishabhh screamed, but instead of dropping to the ground, we floated towards the computer.

Rishabhh was the first to be, I suppose, transmitted into the Internet, or the computer's hard disk. I saw him drop lower and lower until his nose almost touched the computer screen, and he disappeared inch by inch into it. I thought of many things as I found myself being prepared for transmission: Would we make it back into Rishabhh's apartment? Would the Vikings walk out of the door and leave us inside the Internet? Was the Thruxton HT really inside the Internet? How had Rishabhh been transmitted into the hard drive? Even, was he now rishabhhmehtaa.zip?

When it was my turn to be zipped, I was glad that the entire process was a painless one. I felt slightly ticklish for the first few minutes, and rather numb during the rest of my transmission, which, according to my estimate, would have lasted no more than five minutes.

It is quiet and mostly dark inside the Internet, but there were these intermittent shivers of light which provided me with my first glimpse of Chowfin Singh. He wore navy blue overalls that camouflaged his massive paunch, and he carried a leather messenger bag that was strung across his left shoulder.

'I'm here,' I said, walking towards Chowfin and Rishabhh.

'Welcome, welcome. Finally, we meet.'

'It is an honour to meet you.'

'I was just having a chat with Rishabhh. I was very worried when I heard all that commotion. But I'm glad it's all turned out well . . .'

'So far,' I said. 'But I think those guys are on our side.'

'Told you the Velo would think of a way!'

The two of us stood there in bemused silence, while Rishabhh restlessly cracked his knuckles. My eyes swept around the place, but I didn't see the Thruxton HT anywhere. I waited for Chowfin to offer me a ride on the HT.

'So, all set?' he said.

'Yes.' I smiled.

Chowfin put his fat fingers into his mouth and whistled. Somewhere far away something bounced to life. I thought I heard the creak of a rear suspension. Was that the Thruxton HT getting off its centre-stand? I was about to tell Chowfin that maybe he would want to lube up the shock absorbers, when I heard a low rumble that exploded into a tornado of noise, and trapped inside it, like us, were several other creatures, or at least it sounded like that: a woman screamed, a bobcat snarled and, somewhere in the distance, a foghorn moaned.

Once the noise had receded, I saw, in the darkness, the contours of a motorcycle lit up by an intermittent but hostile bioluminescence and heard the distinctive purr of a four-cylinder British motorcycle. The Thruxton HT rode towards Chowfin and halted right beside him. The machine in front of me was not as beautiful or big as the one that had gestated in my imagination for decades – as Jaroslav Vesely said, that engine did seem a bit too large for it – but the HT had an unmistakable, endearing pugnacity about it.

'Look who's here, Velo,' he said, patting its tank.

The motorcycle turned its headlight towards me and when I met its piercing gaze and held it, I got an intimation of what it would feel like to look into the eyes of a murderous lover.

'Come on KK, what are you waiting for?' said Chowfin.

I limbered up and asked Chowfin if there was anything I needed to keep in mind.

'No, no, just have fun. Just be wary of the rear brake, it tends to bite down rather fervently.'

I thanked Chowfin, got on to the HT, and pulled the compression release lever on the underside of the left handlebar and kick-started the bike. A massive explosion filled the air, and the Thruxton HT roared to life, sounding like boulders rolling down a mountain.

I rode gingerly for the first couple of kilometres, as I always do when I'm riding someone else's bike, which, of course, has been the story of my life.

From the way the gears fall into place and the amount of play on the clutch lever to the way the shock absorbers are set and the chicken strips on the tyres, a motorcycle can tell you a lot about its owner. But the Thruxton HT was inscrutable in that regard. Chowfin Singh, the world's greatest rider, had seemingly not left any sort of imprint on it. In fact, from the way the handlebar was angled – I like to crouch a lot more than most riders – to the placement of the foot pegs to the throttle response, it appeared as if it had been customized for me, a sort of KK Swamy special edition of the Thruxton HT, if you please. In a way, it also reminded me of the TMV 4721, Koman's Enfield, the motorcycle that made me the rider I am today. Encouraged by the intimacy I felt with the HT, I went bam! Big mistake. I got instantly pummelled by massive G-forces – over 180Gs for sure, both lateral and longitudinal – and fainted.

When I woke up, I found myself draped on the HT in the middle of a great plain on a golden morning. A swift wind blew across the pale golden grassland,

and a pony grazed not too far from us. Two eagles hovered high above us, and a marmot peeked out of its burrow before disappearing inside. All of a sudden, the pony bolted in alarm and the eagles screeched as the grassland trembled and a gigantic cloud of dust rose on the horizon. I heard the hooves of what seemed to be a million horses pounding the earth. Evidently, whatever was coming at me was an army. I panicked and revved the Thruxton HT up, but the motorcycle refused to budge.

The stocky horses and their riders advanced rapidly towards the centre of the plain, and I saw war banners, lances, battleaxes and bows. The army then discharged a barrage of arrows at us, several of which missed me by inches, even as others embedded themselves into the Thruxton HT's saddle.

The cavalrymen were now so close I could discern the menacing faces of the men who were galloping towards us. They had Oriental features, they wore coats of mail, and they were led by a heavyset man with a Genghis Khan beard. They looked like Mongols. Were we in Mongolia? And the man with the Genghis Khan beard? He looked like . . . was it really him? Of course, it was him. What was he doing here? Off to ransack Europe?

About twenty-five yards separated the HT and me

from annihilation. Genghis reined in his horse as he approached us, curious about the metal contraption and its rider who stood in his path.

He signalled his men to encircle us. I was about to make a run for it when I heard the HT revving itself up and I was on it in a flash. I opened the HT's throttle, and simultaneously turned around to see the Great Khan's face darken. He uttered a blood-curdling war cry, and one of the ancient world's greatest, most efficient and ruthless armies was on my tail. To borrow a cliché from the pages of *Turbo*, I went across the grassland like stink. Genghis and his men chased us over little hills, shallow lakes and, as we rode further, across arid land. The boom of the HT's exhaust note collided with the feral war cries of the Mongols. I rode like never before. I scythed my way through tall grass, and leapt over icy little streams and over startled herds of wild horses. That morning's ride was better than the 7:31 at Petrol Salim's.

The distance between us and our pursuers increased steadily, but Genghis was not one to give up. As evening fell, we approached a river as wide as an ocean. A dense fog hung over the other side of the river. As those thundering hooves closed in, I gauged the breadth of the river, patted the Thruxton's tank and accelerated. We shot towards the water at an alarming pace. The Thruxton slid around on the wet ground, but I managed to catch the slides and powered on. Four metres from the water, I literally heaved the motorcycle off the ground and pointed it towards the sky, and we floated over the river, while on the opposite bank a super moon illuminated the ruthless conqueror's stupefied face.

We sank into the fog and landed with a soft thud. The Thruxton HT idled softly. I thought of riding ahead, but visibility was poor and the motorcycle's headlight merely bounced off the sheets of fog the place appeared to be swaddled in. Once again I waited for something to happen, and it did. A light wind burrowed its way into the fog, dispersed the haze and swept it away, and I found myself standing in a thoroughfare under a blue sky, with natives in loincloth staring expectantly at me. They fell to their knees when they saw me astride the motorcycle.

I avoided their gaze and looked ahead at a massive golden temple that stood at the end of the thoroughfare, an immense pyramid with a flight of stairs that led to the top. A gunshot rang out, and the bullet grazed the HT's tank. I turned around and saw a bunch of armed pale-skinned men leading a tall, brown-skinned man, who wore a bright headdress made of the feathers of some exotic bird, towards the temple. One of his captors, a dwarf with heavy-lidded eyes, like those of an iguana, cocked his musket and aimed it at us. We bolted and wove our way through the throng of natives who ran helter-skelter. More shots rang out, but fortunately, they missed us. We rode up the flight of stairs of the temple and kept going until we reached the shrine at the top. Two startled priests tried to bar my way inside, but we smashed down the wooden doors, knocked down an animal mummy – a platypus, I think – from its pedestal inside the sanctum sanctorum, and dropped down on to a smooth, broad highway that cut through a vast desertscape. The road that meandered through the brown sands was punctuated with milestones, each of which had a kind of hieroglyph etched on it: a king, a mountain and a piano. None of it made any sense, so I got off the motorcycle and contemplated my next course of action. Should I ride ahead, or would the HT take charge? The answer presented itself the next moment, in the form of shrill cries and more gunshots. The pale-skinned men, including the dwarf, had followed me through the maw of the idol and were now coming after me. Right behind them was Genghis and his bloodthirsty horde.

I scrambled on to the motorcycle and sped away until the desert ended at the foot of a mountain. A castle that looked straight out of a fairy tale stood perched on one of its flanks. I gunned it and rode up a steep incline, lined with fir and pine trees. The weather was bracing and after the heat and dust of the desert, I enjoyed the fresh air and the mild off-roading that the trail provided. The huge ornate gates of the castle opened of their own accord, and I entered a beautiful garden surrounded by a walled courtyard. There was no one around, except for two gentlemen. One of them, dressed in regal finery, sat on a bench with his eyes shut. The other was at a piano placed in the centre of the garden.

Neither of them seemed to be aware of our presence.

Upon a nod from the gentleman on the bench, the pianist started his performance. It was a soaring tune. The pianist's sole audience immersed himself in the music. From time to time, the heavily moustachioed gentleman smiled sadly. The grand notes flooded the garden in waves, one after another, and rose through the air, over the courtyard and high above the castle. It was a rousing score. The Thruxton HT rose slowly and floated gently towards the sky, as if it, too, was moved by the music. I held its handlebars tight and watched as a mountainous panorama unfurled itself, and the turrets of the castle faded from view.

We went higher and yet higher until I could grasp the earth in its entirety, and then higher still until we were suspended in space, like the millions of stars around us. For some reason, though, I could still hear the pianist's performance: he was now playing a showy cadenza that exploded into an inferno of music. Then six more chords, and then silence, in which I heard the universe's sad sigh, at the tail end of which the HT launched itself into hyperdrive.

This time, though, I was prepared for the mind-, time- and space-bending acceleration, and followed Chowfin Singh's – and Koman's – advice on riding fast: you go where you look. I also kept the motorcycle's engine on the boil and ran real wide, braking as late as was possible, around the rims of galaxies, and, I think, the glittering, hazy curvature of space–time itself. Towards the end of my third hot lap around the universe, two comets appeared out of nowhere and, acting as pace setters, escorted us deeper and deeper into space.

I didn't know it then, but we were headed towards the heart of a faraway galaxy, into the maw of a supermassive black hole. I'm hopeless at maths and consequently physics, so I have no idea how I managed to survive once I breached the event horizon. But for the benefit of motorcyclists everywhere, here's what you've got to remember if you ever find yourself inside one. At a certain point, everything, and I mean everything around you, will just go bam! and your motorcycle will go into a violent slide. What should you do next? More power is always the answer – wring that throttle wide open. You will eventually find traction and discover that riding towards – and hopefully past – the fatal singularity is a lot like riding in the wet. As Chowfin said, the trick to make it out of a black hole is to go faster than everything around you, faster than the pull of the damn thing, but, even as you attempt to do that, you've got to keep all your inputs – clutch, brake, throttle – smooth. Use your rear brake more often but brake hard all the same, and enter bends just that bit slower than you normally would.

Black holes are, of course, quiet places, which helps you focus, but towards the centre one should expect a lot of static noises, and that is the cue to accelerate even harder. The HT's 'infinite gearing' helped here. I must have shifted through at least a thousand gears before I blasted out of the other side of that wicked vortex of nothingness. When I did that I saw light again for a brief instant, and then darkness fell over us. But I kept riding, and from the texture of the surface beneath the motorcycle's tyres, I realized we were back inside the Internet.

The Internet is mostly smooth and straight, but there are some gentle sweepers where you can hang really low. I realized my time with the HT was coming to an end when someone waved a giant chequered flag and I heard cheering all around. Floodlights came on from nowhere and illuminated the faces of throngs of racegoers and motorcycle lovers. Among them, I saw the familiar faces of Koman and Gopi, and I obliged them by pulling a really long wheelie, and then power-slided dirt-bike style before coming to a halt near Chowfin Singh and Rishabhh.

'Welcome back, welcome back,' said Chowfin.

'God, that was madness. Extreme stuff.'

Chowfin smiled. 'I know better than to ask you for details,' he said, as he removed a couple of arrows that were still embedded in the HT's seat, inspected the deep dent caused by the pale guy's bullet, and wiped some cosmic dust off the tank and the rims of the motorcycle's wheels.

'I don't know how to thank you, Chowfin. I–'

'I'm the one who should be thanking you – and please stay seated on the bike.'

'You mean I should be taking the Velo for another spin?' I said and laughed.

'Of course you should! Go right ahead! In fact, you can now ride the Velocette, I suppose, forever. It's yours,' Chowfin said. His voice sagged a bit.

'What? Chowfin!'

Chowfin took a deep breath and composed himself. He walked up to the motorcycle and patted its fuel tank and wiped its odometer with a frayed piece of cloth.

'I've been riding the Velo for over, what, forty years? You know, I never thought I'd ride it to my heart's content. Never thought I'll be able to do what I'm about to do today, but this is it. I don't think there's any place left on the earth or elsewhere where I haven't ridden. I've had lots of fun. So much fun. But yes, it's time to make way for someone who's been chosen by the Velo itself . . .'

'No, no, no–'

I felt conflicted about the whole thing. On the one hand, I was thinking about zero to 1000 kph in 3.8 seconds, massive burnouts that would destroy continents, wheeling all the way to Jupiter, and general, uncompromising hooliganism. But on the other, I felt that the Velo and Chowfin were entwined together forever, like Joey Dunlop and his Honda RC30, or Sebastien Loeb and his Citroen C4 WRC. Who was I to creep into this relationship?

Chowfin raised his hand, and when I piped down, he said, 'I've always wanted to lead an interesting life, KK – not necessarily a happy one, or a peaceful one, or, you know, a regular life, with kids and a job and things like that. I'm glad I've done that. My life, nearly my entire life, has been one incredible ride. But, as wondrous as it was, what's a great ride if you can't share your story with another passionate motorcyclist? I'm not much of a philosopher but that's among the big reasons why we ride – we meet people along the way, and we tell each other where we're coming from and where we are going. But I always wondered about who'd believe me. Sitting here and chatting with you, it makes me feel so good. It makes me feel like my ride is finally complete. I know you will do justice to the Velo, and I'm certain you and Rishabhh here will let the world know about the greatest motorcycle that ever roamed the earth.'

'Chowfin, Chowfin. All of what you've said makes sense, but what will you do without the Velo? We can ride together! I'll borrow the Velo from you whenever I feel like I need some excitement in my life. Come on, let's go.'

Chowfin smiled.

'I'll just spend some time here. It's peaceful and quiet, perfect for an old man like me. I'll walk a bit, and maybe just lie down around the corner. I hope the rest of my life is a short one. I will go now. Goodbye. Thank you once again.'

The Thruxton stood there impassively as Chowfin planted a kiss on its tank, and disappeared into the darkness.

'Chowfin, wait! Listen . . .' I kick-started the Velo, but it wouldn't budge. I got off the bike in order to chase Chowfin on foot, but the Velo turned around, barred my way and snarled at me.

'Dude, this thing is mad. Chill.'

The next instant, I found myself being lifted off the ground along with Rishabhh and the Velo, and soon the three of us descended slowly, one after the another, into Bluetooth's massive arms.

The Viking king looked quizzically at the motorcycle, and grunted, before placing it on the floor. He then grunted again and walked off. His men followed him, but just as they were nearing the door, one of the men turned around and walked up to me.

He grabbed me by my neck.

'The name of my king is Harald Blatand, aka Bluetooth, yes? Remember, yes?' he said.

I smiled obsequiously as the Viking warrior walked out of the door.

17

I don't know if you've read the works of the great mountaineer and explorer H.W. 'Bill' Tilman, but you should really get your hands on his *The Ascent of Nanda Devi*, which remains one of my favourite books to this day. The reason I bring this up here is because something in the book resonated strongly with me. In August of 1936, after becoming the first man to summit the magnificent mountain, Tilman wrote, 'I remember, in the small hours, when the spark of life burns lowest, the feeling which predominated over all was one of remorse at the fall of a giant. It is the same sort of contrition that one feels at the shooting of an elephant, for however thrilling and arduous the chase, however great has been the call upon skill, perseverance and endurance, and however gratifying the weight of the ivory, when the great bulk crashes to the ground achievement seems to have been bought at the too high cost of sacrilege.'

For many years, as I plunged deeper and deeper into the abyss of my obsession and all through my rabid pursuit of the Thruxton HT, I wondered if, I, too, would encounter the emptiness of accomplishment, so to speak, after finally riding – and taming – the world's greatest motorcycle. Nothing of that sort happened, though, and I even felt a bit disappointed that I had experienced no such noble emotion. I suppose I'm a bit crude that way, and all I wanted to do was raise hell with the Thruxton HT. But I have to add here that it did take me some time to come to terms with Chowfin Singh's sudden, unexpected departure. It would have been an instructive experience to ride in the slipstream of the greatest rider the world has ever seen, and while this might sound odd – and I'm sure motorcyclists everywhere will understand this – I do hope the rest of his life was a short one.

Just before I left Bombay, I finished a suitably filtered 4,354-word article on our chase of the Thruxton HT for Rishabhh. I left, as I was advised, the reader 'hanging' – on the flight back from Calcutta, Rishabhh realizes that regardless of the number of fast bikes he rides for the rest of his life, he will always wonder whether he would have been good enough for a monster British bike that has been lost to history.

Our parting was rather abrupt. I told him I couldn't thank him enough, but all he wanted was for me to vanish. I'll admit here that I was a bit taken aback; towards the end of our journey together, I'd even begun to like that space cadet. But, I suppose, getting the fuck out of his life was the best way to repay my gratitude.

I have mostly been riding non-stop since then and have seen some real cool-ass shit, but, in case you're wondering, there has been no sign of any other god yet, which means that perhaps I'm the only god around, and that I may have been searching for myself all this while. (Fuck, I just realized that last line makes me sound distressingly like Deepak Chopra or Paulo Coelho.) I do miss Kollengode at times, though, but up here, wrenched out of my context, I also feel strangely liberated.

All that matters at the moment is to keep moving. And how can I not when everything around me – galaxies, voids, super voids, stars, asteroids and the entire goddamn universe itself – is moving, accelerating away. Where are all these things going? As always I have no clue, but I'm hot on their tail.

Acknowledgements

My parents came to Bombay in the late 1960s, but they never really left Kollengode, an idyllic village in Kerala where the water is sweet, the nights are dark and everyone, I've always thought, talks a bit too much. This story is born out of the stories my parents told my sister and me when we were children.

Several other people helped shape this book. These include my sister Sushi, and friends and former colleagues such as Harneet Singh, Srinivas Krishnan, Shubhabrata Marmar, Sameer Kumar, Adil Jal Darukhanawala, Jaya Peter, Dwijottam Bhattacharjee, Meenal Baghel, Kyle Pereira, Kartik Ware and Bijoy Kumar Y. I would also like to thank my indefatigable agent Kanishka Gupta and my editors at Juggernaut: R. Sivapriya, Chiki Sarkar, Sasha Mahuli and Cincy Jose.

AN EXTENSIVE LIBRARY

Including fresh, new, original Juggernaut books from the likes of Sunny Leone, Praveen Swami, Husain Haqqani, Umera Ahmed, Rujuta Diwekar and lots more. Plus, books from partner publishers and loads of free classics. Whichever genre you like, there's a book waiting for you.

CRUCIBLES OF SIN
HITESHA
Can a Geek ever find Love?
Finding Juliet
Toffee
Mary Shelley
Frankenstein
A FAROOQ BASHI INVESTIGATION
COLD FLAKE
PRAVEEN SWAMI
A Psychiatrist's Guide To Heartbreak
How to Heal Your Broken Heart
DR SHYAM BHAT
MOIN and THE MONSTER
ANUSHKA RAVISHANKAR
Mafia Queens of Mumbai
Stories of women from the ganglands
S. Hussain Zaidi with Jane Borges
Foreword by Vishal Bharadwaj
Pakistan's Queen of Romance
UMERA AHMED
Nowhere Girl
A Story of Love & Forgiveness
THE BEHEADING
This Is How He Will Bless Her
ABHEEK BARUA
THE Peshwa
The Lion and the Stallion
THE INVISIBLE WOMAN
SAURBH KATYAL
ANGRY BIRDS FAN? READ THE BOOK!
ANGRY BIRDS TOONS
TOONS TALES
ARCHANA SABOO
ADIKOOL
in
#AfricanAdventures
i am not a bimbette
Tarana Khan
She hates me, He loves me not but...
DON'T FALL IN LOVE
Vandana Shankar
KHUSHWANT SINGH
WE INDIANS

Ask authors questions

Get all your answers from the horse's mouth. Juggernaut authors actually reply to every question they can.

Rate and review

Let everyone know of your favourite reads or critique the finer points of a book – you will be heard in a community of like-minded readers.

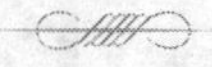

Gift books to friends

For a book-lover, there's no nicer gift than a book personally picked. You can even do it anonymously if you like.

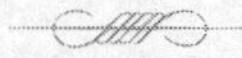

Enjoy new book formats

Discover serials released in parts over time, picture books including comics, and story-bundles at discounted rates. And coming soon, audiobooks.

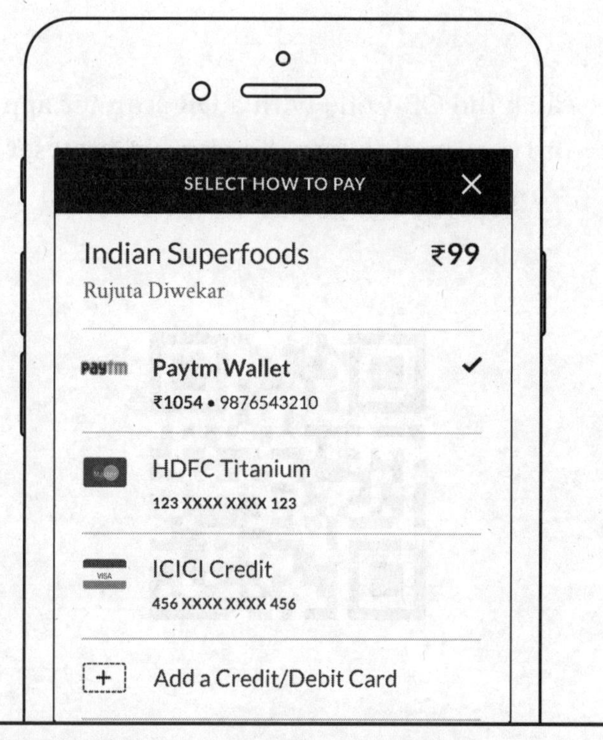

Paytm Wallet, Cards & Apple Payments

On Android, just add a Paytm Wallet once and buy any book with one tap. On iOS, pay with one tap with your iTunes-linked debit/credit card.

Click the QR Code with a QR scanner app
or type the link into the Internet browser
on your phone to download the app.